D0504577

University of the
West of England
BRISTOL

This book

GHOSTLY
TALES FOR
GHASTLY
KIDS

Stories by Jamie Rix
Illustrated by Bobbie Spargo

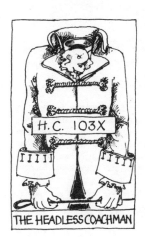

André Deutsch Children's Books

Scholastic Children's Books,
Scholastic Publications Ltd,
7–9 Pratt Street, London NW1 0AE, UK

Scholastic Inc.,
730 Broadway, New York, NY 10003, USA

Scholastic Canada Ltd,
123 Newkirk Road, Richmond Hill,
Ontario, Canada L4C 3G5

Ashton Scholastic Pty Ltd,
P O Box 579, Gosford, New South Wales,
Australia

Ashton Scholastic Ltd,
Private Bag 1, Penrose, Auckland,
New Zealand

First published in the UK by Scholastic Publications Ltd, 1992

Text copyright © 1992 by Jamie Rix
Illustrations copyright © 1992 by Bobbie Spargo

ISBN 0 590 54004 1

Typeset by Contour Typesetters, Southall, London

All rights reserved.

The author, Jamie Rix, has asserted his moral right to be
identified as the author of the work

10 9 8 7 6 5 4 3 2 1

This book is sold subject to the condition that it shall not, by
way of trade or otherwise be lent, resold, hired out, or
otherwise circulated without the publisher's prior consent in
any form of binding or cover other than that in which it is
published and without a similar condition, including this
condition, being imposed upon the subsequent purchaser.

REDLAND LIBRARY
UNIVERSITY OF THE WEST OF
ENGLAND, BRISTOL
REDLAND HILL
BRISTOL BS6 6UZ

Contents

For Helen
The only person I know who
has actually met a ghost

Grandmother's Footsteps

I couldn't sleep. There was a man outside my bedroom window. He was a huge man with long black fingernails and wild grey hair. He was trying to get me to let him in, but I wouldn't. He talked to me in a soft, whispering voice about a magic far off land where trees were made out of bread sticks and the lakes were full of humus. He said he'd take me there if only I'd open the window, but I wouldn't. He promised me a ride on a flying carpet and a yacht that could sail to the moon if only I'd let him in out of the cold, but I wouldn't. I was too scared.

He might have been a ghost.

So I lay there for most of the night just listening to his fingers tapping on the window pane, until finally I plucked up enough courage to speak. "Grandmaaaa!" I shouted. And Grandma came running.

When I told her that there was a ghost outside my window, she laughed.

"But I heard it," I said. "Listen." We listened to the

tapping and she laughed some more. "And I've seen it," I added, pointing to the shadow that loomed through my curtain.

My Grandma stopped laughing and said, "I'm going to tell you a story."

"Oh," I said, but I didn't let her see how surprised I was, in case she changed her mind.

"This is a ghost story," said Grandma, pulling me up onto her knee. The smell of mothballs was so strong it made me cough. Her boney fingers poked into my ribs as she plumped me up and down like a lumpy cushion. Her cold, dry lips pressed against my cheek. There would be a thin red circle of lipstick there in the morning. I wiped my cheek with the sleeve of my pyjamas and settled down to listen.

"There was a boy," she said, "not much older than you.

2

His name was Jolyon, and he lived in a huge draughty old house by the edge of a lake."

"Is he the ghost?" I asked.

"No," said my grandmother, "not Jolyon. His bedroom was right at the top of the house, in a dark dark room that had once been full to the ceiling with spiders, earwigs and big black beetles."

I pulled the shawl off her shoulders and tucked it into my ears. I felt safer when her voice was ever so slightly muffled.

"Go on," I said. "This boy who looked like me was in his spooky old bedroom and there was a ghost . . ."

"Not yet," said Grandma.

"A ghost behind the door," I squealed, "a mad, ranting blood-sucking ghost waiting to stuff a straw into Jolyon's head and suck his brains out like a banana milkshake."

"No," said Grandma.

"It's an under-the-bed ghost then!"

"The ghost hasn't turned up yet."

"But there will be one?"

"As sure as day turns to night," she assured me. "Now, this boy Jolyon . . ."

My grandmother drew me closer, and wound her chicken-bone arms tightly across my chest. "He was in his bedroom, reading a dusty old book by the light of a small, white, guttering candle . . ."

"A ghost book?" I said.

"No," said my grandmother, "the ghost comes later . . . Suddenly the candle spluttered and went out. At first Jolyon could see nothing, but as his eyes adjusted to the moonlight he could vaguely make out a tall thin shadowy figure outside his window."

3

"The ghost!" I yelled.

"Not yet," said Grandma. "It was then that Jolyon heard the scratching. It was there for just a fraction of a second, but it was enough to make him sit bolt upright in bed and hold his breath. He waited to a count of ten. He heard nothing more and breathed again. The second time the scratching was louder."

"Is it the ghost, Grandma?" I asked from underneath her shawl.

"No, dear. Be patient. Just wait and see." Grandma made a funny clicking noise with her teeth and carried on. "Jolyon was underneath the bedclothes in a flash. A ghostly hand was scratching at his window! Five boney fingers trying to get into *his* bedroom! He was as good as dead. His mouth was dry. His shiny, white knuckles stood out in the gloom under his blankets.

Then the scratching stopped.

There was a deadly silence.

Jolyon gasped. He closed his eyes and wished with all his might that his ghostly visitor might go away. He wished and wished and wished and . . . Rat-a-tat-tat. Rat-a-tat-tat . . . It was then that the knocking started."

"It is the ghost!" I shouted, holding tightly onto Grandma's shawl.

"It is not," she said, stroking my hair. "The ghost comes at the end, but Jolyon doesn't know that, because he's in the story. All he can hear is the knocking. All he can see is the shadow lurking outside the window. All he can smell is the fear. *His* fear, fugging up under his bedclothes."

Grandma took out her left eye and polished it.

"Well go on," I said, impatiently.

"Jolyon lay in his bed, terrified to move lest this huge beastly skeleton should leap into the room and chop him up with an axe. He lay quite still, for hours on end, watching the shadow growing larger and larger, coming closer and closer. Until suddenly, there was a terrible crash of glass as the giant fingers smashed in through the window. Jolyon screamed. He felt a cold rush of air as the ghostly shadow sprang across the room towards him. It was then that the door to his bedroom burst open . . ."

"This *must* be the ghost," I yelped.

"No," said my grandmother. "Not long now though. It was Jolyon's grandmother, bouncing into his bedroom, wielding a copper bedpan. She had heard his screams for help and had leapt from her bed to protect him. Jolyon was curled up under his blankets.

'Don't let the ghost get me,' he sobbed. 'Don't let the ghost chop me up and eat me!'"

I looked at Grandma and she looked straight back at me.

"But you said it wasn't a ghost outside the window."

"It wasn't," she replied. "The tapping was just the wind, blowing the branches from an apple tree against the window. Then the wind became a storm, and the branches battered the glass until it smashed. It was Jolyon's imagination that created the ghost."

I asked her if that was what had happened to me. She said she thought it probably was.

"Oh," I said, feeling rather small and embarrassed. Then I added, "If Jolyon's ghost was not a real ghost after all, then you lied to me."

5

"Did I?" said my grandmother.

"You said that you were going to tell me a ghost story."

"And so I did."

"And you definitely said that the ghost would appear at the end."

"That's right," said my grandmother. "And here I am."

She stopped at the door and removed her head to rest her tired shoulders.

Then she just disappeared, and I was sure I heard her ghostly footsteps treading a path back into a different world.

I didn't sleep for a week after that.

Burgers

The air was filled with whooping and yelling. The ground shook to the sound of thundering feet and a vast dust cloud billowed out behind the stampeding herd. With nostrils flared and mad panic in their eyes the school-children bumped and jostled each other as they swept out of the coach and poured in through the doors of Burgerskip. They laughed to see the smiling, white face of the fifty foot clown which towered over the entrance and bade them welcome. It was the face of Seamus O'Burger, the man who had created Burgerskip. His cardboard look-alike surveyed this scene of hysterical greed, and beamed from cut-out ear to cut-out ear. Though nobody knew it, it was the smile of death.

Just another day in Crawley High Street. Just one day closer to the complete obliteration of the planet Earth.

Meanwhile somewhere in South America, a herd of *real* cattle grazed in a clearing on long lush grass, unaware that Seamus O'Burger had already decided their fate. In his factory, row upon row of little brown polystyrene coffins lay waiting for them, lids agape. Next door, jars of pickled cucumbers, shreds of lettuce and crispy, burnt buns sat in readiness, and beyond them was the slaughter house, Seamus's favourite haunt, where the cattle would be smothered to death with lashings of tomato ketchup.

Yet, disgusting though this was, Seamus's evil plan for world domination through the minds and stomachs of its children was having a far more sinister effect. In his bid for global expansion Seamus was sacrificing the heart and lungs of the planet. The Amazonian Rain Forest.

The helicopter swooped low over the tree tops brushing the very highest branches with its floats.

"Down there," shouted the pilot to the clown sitting beside him.

"What is?" shouted Seamus back, trying to make himself heard above the noise of the engine.

"The greenest, most fertile land you'll find for thousands of miles," said the pilot.

"But it's all trees!"

"It *is* a forest," replied the pilot, "what do you expect?"

"I can't graze my cattle on twigs and branches!" screamed Seamus aggressively. "They need wide open spaces."

"So?" said the pilot. "Cut all the trees down."

"I know," said Seamus, who like all evil masterminds had to be the first to think up good ideas, "I'll cut all the trees down and graze my cattle there."

"I wish I'd thought of that," said the pilot.

Seamus's eyes lit up with pound signs as the helicopter climbed steeply and headed for home.

A family of monkeys, frightened by the screaming engines of the metal bird, leapt for safety. The smallest of them, only three weeks old, did not have the strength to jump as far as his parents and plummeted onto the forest floor below. When his mother found him his neck was broken and he was quite dead.

The next day the bulldozers moved in. Seamus needed more space to fatten up more cattle, because more cattle meant more burgers, and more burgers meant more money. Sadly though, more money did not make Seamus any nicer a person.

The forest was a beautiful place. For hundreds of years the trees had been left to grow in peace and now they threw open their arms offering safe havens to all the thousands of animals that lived beneath them. Flowers, like nothing you have ever seen before (or are ever likely to see again), blossomed in a rainbow of breathtaking colours, and glistening streams, bringing life to everything they touched, nattered constantly to each other as they flowed down to the mighty Amazon River.

At the centre of this untouched paradise stood the tallest tree in the forest. The Amazonian Indians called it "Panachek", which roughly translated means God. It was a huge three hundred foot Mahogany tree, which, so legend told, was possessed of magical powers. From its roots ran the roots of every other tree in the forest, and the Indians believed that if Panachek should die, then the whole forest would die with it.

Seamus O'Burger was driving the biggest bulldozer. He screamed with delight as he thrust the lever forward. The giant claw on the front of his machine chewed a path through the undergrowth and crashed pitilessly into the nearest tree. There was a cry of pain as the roots were torn from the ground, but Seamus didn't hear it. He put his foot down hard and drove on towards the centre of the forest. His caterpillar tracks biting into the fallen trunk and making it bleed.

For days on end all that could be heard in the forest was the sound of men shouting, trees falling, chainsaws buzzing and Seamus O'Burger counting his money.

Seamus's forest guide was an Amazonian Indian. He had not realised the full extent of Seamus's evil plan until it was too late.

"I want to go back," he said one morning.

"Nonsense," snapped Seamus. "You can't! You'll go when I say so and not before."

The guide hung his head and mumbled something about "Panachek".

"Speak up!" shouted Seamus as he sank his teeth into a Burgerskip Big Beef Breakfast Bap.

"That tree over there," said the guide, pointing to a magnificent, three hundred foot Mahogany, "is Panachek. If you cut it down you will bring the whole world tumbling around your ears."

"Mumbo Jumbo," sneered Seamus, adjusting his red nose. "It's just a tree. Cut it down!" he shouted to his men who were busy cleaning their saws.

"No!" pleaded the guide, sinking to his knees in front of Seamus. "You don't know what you're doing!"

Seamus swept past the guide and knocked him to the forest floor. "Pull it down!" he screamed again. "Pull it down, and bring me its highest branch as a trophy!"

The lumberjacks seemed reluctant to carry out Seamus's orders.

"What is it now?" said Seamus.

The leader of the lumberjacks stepped forward. "We are afraid," he said. "There is much magic in that tree. We dare not touch it!"

Seamus was in no mood to argue. "Then *I* shall!" he fumed, grabbing the nearest chainsaw and striding off towards the Mahogany tree all by himself.

As the teeth of the saw sank into the bark an ominous silence fell over the forest. The birds had stopped squawking. The animals had stopped moving. The forest was holding its breath. The chainsaw gouged the first lump of wood out of Panachek's side and the mighty tree let out a groan. To you or me it would have sounded like the creaking of a branch, but it *was* a groan. Sap poured

out of the cut in a vain attempt to heal the wound, but Seamus was taking no prisoners. He cut deeper and deeper. The rest of the forest was now in tune with Panachek's pain. All the flowers closed their petals, creepers shrivelled and leaves started falling from the trees. Then slowly, as Seamus brought Panachek's life closer and closer to its end, a low mournful wailing spread far and wide across the tree tops as the forest exhaled its final breath.

Panachek crashed to the ground and Seamus stood triumphant by its severed stump.

"Now," he said, "I can graze my cattle!"

"Yes," said the guide, "but the forest is dead."

Seamus O'Burger made a lot of burgers out of the extra cattle that he was able to graze in his clearing. So many burgers, in fact, that soon he was feeding the entire population of Great Britain with them. Unfortunately, though, there are a lot of people in Great Britain, and Seamus quickly discovered that he was fast running out of land on which to feed his enormous herd of cattle. He went up in the helicopter again to look for new areas of the Rain Forest to knock down.

And he would have found some, had not the most extraordinary event taken place that very same day in Crawley High Street.

A rather unpleasant young girl called Charlotte had been pestering her father all day for a Burgerskip Jolly Burger. "With chips!" she kept adding, in case he hadn't got the message.

Her father had finally relented, as all weak parents tend

to do. They had duly driven down to Burgerskip in Crawley High Street and purchased a Jolly Burger, complete with free Seamus O'Burger 'smiley face-mask'. Outside in the street, such was her greed, Charlotte tore off the countless wrappings, dropping them all on the pavement, closed her eyes in sheer unadulterated delight, and sank her teeth into the bun.

"Urgh!" she suddenly screamed. "Puh! Puh! Puh!" She spat bits of burger all over the road.

"Charlotte what are you doing!" yelled her father, who was more than a little embarrassed.

"There's a tree in my Jolly Burger!" she wailed.

"A tree!" said her father, snatching the soggy bun from her mouth. He opened it up and took a step backwards in surprise. She was right. There, sticking up, in the middle of Charlotte's Jolly Burger, was a tiny Mahogany tree. It was only one and a half inches tall, but it was a tree alright!

Seamus O'Burger heard the news in his helicopter. It was flashed over the two-way radio, which linked him, at all times, with his own headquarters. "A tree in a Jolly Burger! It's unthinkable! Turn this thing around!" he shouted to the pilot. "If the press get hold of this story, I'm ruined!"

Back in the offices of Burgerskip, Seamus's team of burger experts were quaking in their boots.

"He'll sack us all for sure," said one.

"It's not my fault," said another. "I just make the boxes."

"Well, where did the tree come from?" said a third, who was hiding under the boardroom table. Just then, Seamus burst into the room. His eyes were blazing with anger, and tiny flecks of white spittle dribbled from the corners of his mouth. He tore off his spinning bowtie, hurled his red nose into the bin and wiped the clown make-up off his face with his spotty red handkerchief.

"Gentlemen," he snarled, "you have let me down. All of you! Find me the culprit! Find me the imbecile who planted a tree in Charlotte's Jolly Burger!"

A nervous hand went up at the back of the room.

"What?" screamed Seamus.

"Mr O'Burger, sir," quivered the tiny voice," erm . . . I'm afraid . . . erm . . . that it's not *just* Charlotte's anymore."

You could have heard a pin drop. The man gulped and went on. "In the past hour, there have been reports of Mahogany trees growing in Jolly Burgers up and down the country. It seems to be happening everywhere." The little man burst into hysterical sobs. "Don't hit me!" he squealed, as Seamus rose slowly from his chair. Steam was coming out of the trick rose on his lapel.

"If I was King Henry VIIIth, I'd send you all to the tower and have your miserable little heads cut off!"

There was a knock at the door. They all looked round. There was another knock.

"Go away!" shouted Seamus, but the knocking continued. Then suddenly the door swung open.

"What do *you* want?" said Seamus testily. "Get out!"

"I should have made you listen before," said the figure in the doorway. "This time you *will* listen!"

It was the forest guide who had tried to stop Seamus from harming the mighty Mahogany tree, Panachek.

"I have come to tell you exactly what you have done," said the guide walking into the room.

"I chopped down a tree!" said Seamus casually.

"You killed Panachek. You murdered the rain forest, and all in the name of greed. Now you will pay the price. It is written that whomsoever defiles the God Panachek, shall be haunted by its ghost until he too is dead!"

"But I'm not dead" taunted Seamus.

"Maybe not you, personally, Mr Seamus 'smiley-face' O'Burger, but your company, Burgerskip *is*! Take a look outside."

Seamus Macburger's face fell so far when he looked out of the window that he was never able to smile again. Where once had been a Burgerskip restaurant, now stood not one Mahogany tree, but thousands. Thousands more were springing up even as he watched. Cars had been abandoned and people fled in terror as three hundred foot

15

trees tore through the tarmac as if it were no more than tissue paper.

"This is a trick!" screamed Seamus.

"No trick," said the guide. "Justice. You destroy our lives. Panachek will destroy yours. This is happening all over the country, Mr O'Burger, to every single one of your restaurants."

Seamus O'Burger was a desperate man, and desperate men do stupid things. He leapt forward in a mad frenzy and grabbed the guide around his neck. "You will pay for this!" he ranted, squeezing as hard as he could, "You can't destroy Seamus O'Burger!"

A terrible rumbling shook the boardroom. The brightly coloured portraits of the clown tyrant fell off the wall, and just as the guide thought he would surely suffocate, the ghost of Panachek burst through the floorboards, scooped up Seamus O'Burger in its twisted branches, and climbed up and up towards the sky.

Seamus O'Burger was never seen again. An Australian farmer found a clown's waistcoat in his pig's trough some years later, but nobody could prove that it belonged to Seamus, despite the relish stains down the front. Burger-skip never sold another burger, which meant, incidentally, that the streets became litter-free. Charlotte became a vegetarian, and Britain, due to the fact that it was now the proud owner of the largest Rain Forest in the world, noticed a slight alteration in its weather pattern.

Oh yes, and roast parrot became as common as roast chicken on people's tables for Sunday lunch.

Tag

Terry Blotch was a spotty child. At the age of nine he had a face like a piece of nutty chocolate. All lumps and bumps and bits of dirty sticking plaster. His parents had tried everything from steam baths to cheese graters, but nothing could quell the mass of heaving eruptions all over his face.

"It might have something to do with his diet," said one doctor. But it didn't.

"It might have something to do with the number of baths he takes," said another. Wrong again.

"How about make up?" said a third. "Do you wear it?"

Terry Blotch laughed until his nose nearly burst. "Make up," he blurted, "is for girls, and I am not a girl!"

So it wasn't make up.

Now, before we go any further, I don't want you to start feeling sorry for Terry. I know it must have been awful to look the way he did, but he did bring it all on himself. Six months earlier he had looked just like every other child of his age. Snotty, dirty, scabby, muddy, and dragged backwards through a hedgey. BUT (and this is a big but) there was not a single spot to be seen anywhere.

It all started on the morning of Jonathan Moore's birthday. Jonathan was one of Terry's friends, and for a birthday present he had been given the hugest marble in the world by his Scottish grandmother. It had been delivered the night before by an exhausted postman, who had rolled it five hundred miles from Glasgow.

You can imagine the scene when Jonathan rolled his marble into the school playground. If he had been pushing a giant Malteser he couldn't have had more attention. The children swarmed over it like wasps and Jonathan was the hero of the day. To everyone but Terry.

Have you ever been jealous? Have you ever had that little green worm crawl into your ear and whisper, "Why's he getting all the attention? You're just as nice as him. In fact you're nicer. Natalie's only looking at him like that because he's got a big marble, it's you she really likes. Go on, get in there, make everyone notice you for a change. You deserve it. He doesn't!"

Terry heard that persuasive little voice on the morning Jonathan brought his marble into school. It made him so jealous that all he wanted to do was to hurt his friend, and the only way he could think of doing that, was by stealing something from Jonathan that Jonathan really liked.

While all the other children were preoccupied in the playground Terry slipped back into the classroom. Shutting the door behind him, so that Mr Sissons, their teacher, wouldn't see what he was doing, Terry crept over to Jonathan's desk and opened it. Inside there was a ruler, several rubbers, four broken pencils and a ring with a skull on it. Terry's hand darted out, like the tongue of a chameleon, and before you could shout "Thief!", the ring was snuggling amidst the sticky sweet wrappers in Terry's trouser pocket.

Now as any thief will tell you, the first time that you steal is always the worst. After that it becomes progressively easier. You stop worrying about being caught, and you become more daring with each theft. But each theft feeds your greed. So that six months later, Terry was no longer content to snatch rings with skulls on them. Each time, he wanted something bigger and better than the time before. In his room at home he was amassing quite a treasure trove. Jewellery, bags of sweets, comics, radios, he even had a pet dog for a while, but when the dog started peeing on his bedspread he decided to return it, pronto, to its owner.

One day, while the other children were at break and Terry was in his customary hidey-hole in the locker room, his shifty eyes fell upon a gym bag. He noticed it, because he had never seen it before. It was hanging, all by itself, from a peg high up on the wall. He could not resist taking a look inside it, just in case there was anything worth nicking. The first thing he saw on the bag was a large name tag. "A. PHANTOM" it announced in bold letters. Terry had never heard of a boy called Phantom, but it hardly mattered because inside the bag was a brand new football kit. Just what Terry had always wanted! There was only one problem. The shorts, the shirt, the socks, even the football boots, all had one of these name tags sewn into them. Terry made a snap decision. He wouldn't

worry about it. Then he sauntered out of the locker room with the bag slung cockily over his shoulder as if the football kit had been his all along.

If he'd bothered to look back at the peg, upon which the gym bag had been hanging, he would have seen it disappear in a puff of purple smoke, leaving, in its place, a thin trickle of green slime, which slid down the wall and stripped the paint off a school bench.

Terry's new football kit was much admired by all of his schoolfriends. In fact, I dare say, that little green worm of envy crept into a few of *their* ears when they first saw it. Terry wore it most of the time, and as A. PHANTOM never challenged Terry to return his kit, Terry thought that he had got away with the perfect crime.

What Terry didn't know was that he would never be challenged by A. PHANTOM because A. PHANTOM did not exist. A. PHANTOM was a ghost – an exceedingly

21

law-abiding ghost, who travelled through time and space in a never ending quest to bring thieving children to justice.

It was about this time that Terry started to notice little red marks appearing on his legs, on his waist, and on the back of his neck. He had been aware that the name tags in his new football kit rubbed him slightly whenever he wore it, but this was to be expected. He had never come across a name tag that *didn't* itch. That was partly why mothers sewed them into clothes, he thought, to ensure that their children's knickers were all lumpy and bumpy.

But the red marks would not go away. In fact they got worse.

He started to scratch them in the middle of the night, which was quite the worst thing he could do. They got angrier and angrier, until one morning he woke up to find himself covered in tiny purple lumps.

The doctor took one look at them and declared, "No chocolate, no sugar, no sweets of any description. Sticky buns are out and Coca-Cola is a definite no-no. I want to see you eating greens, lots of them, plenty of fresh fruit, brown bread and a large spoonful of vinegar before every meal."

Terry's face turned a nasty shade of green.

"But, doctor," said Terry's mother, "What's the matter with him?"

"Haven't got a clue," replied the doctor, "but that's what I eat everyday and it's never done me any harm! Next!"

That night in the bath, Terry's mother let out a little scream as she turned Terry round to scrub his back. The purple lumps had spread.

"They're all over your back!" she yelped. "Oh dear! Terry, you haven't been playing with any chickens behind my back, have you?"

"What?" said Terry, who didn't know what his mother was talking about.

"I think it may be chicken pox!"

"It's not chicken pox, Mum. The doctor would have said so."

"It's that football kit!" said his mother suddenly. "Ever since you've been wearing that blessed football kit . . ." She couldn't continue and left the room in floods of tears.

The spots were growing at an alarming rate. Very soon his whole body was covered in a mass of itchy zits that throbbed and pulsated like a set of disco lights. He stopped going to school, because other children's mothers were afraid that his condition might be contagious. Terry just lay in his darkened room wondering why on earth it should happen to him.

One night Terry found out.

He couldn't sleep. The spots itched him more than usual and whenever he scratched one he felt a pop, which was so painful that he had to bite his lip so as not to cry out. He lost count of how many spots popped that night, but, at a guess, I'd say somewhere in the region of one thousand and twenty.

At three o'clock he could bear it no longer. He let out a pathetic wail and cried for his mummy. She came running into the room, tripping over her dressing gown and landing face down in a pool of sticky stuff by his bed. Cue

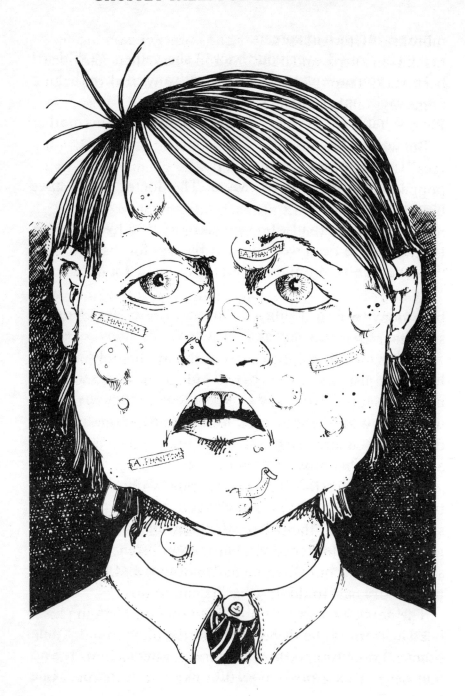

more tears from mother. Her baby was lying on the bed, his skin all purple and bubbling and where there had once been spots there were now one thousand and nineteen name tags, and each one proclaimed, in bold letters, "A. PHANTOM".

But what of the one thousand and twentieth spot. If you recall I said that one thousand and twenty spots had popped that night. Terry's mother found it. It was the biggest name tag of all, stitched into the back of Terry's neck, and on it was printed one word . . . five simple letters:

"THIEF."

"Cut it off!" wailed Terry, as his mother rushed into the bathroom to find a pair of nail scissors. "Unpick the stitches, please!"

Terry's mother snipped away at the stitches for half an hour, but just as soon as she had pulled one out, another magically appeared to take its place. There's only so much unpicking a mother can take. Terry's mother finally laid down her scissors, turned Terry round to face her, and asked him what it was all about.

Terry's confession took a little under an hour to come tumbling out. He told his mother about the ring with the skull on it, about the radios, the bags of sweets and the gym bag in the locker room. His mother listened without saying a word, but when he had finished, and had cried himself dry, she told him what he had to do.

The next day Terry went back to school. He hung his head in shame as he sloped through the playground. The other children stopped shouting and pointed at him. They had never seen a boy covered in name tags before. He went into the building by the side door and slipped past the headteacher's office into the locker room.

Terry checked to see if he was alone, before taking the gym bag out from underneath his jumper. Then, climbing onto a bench he reached up and hung it over the peg on which he had first found it. Quickly, he jumped down and ran out of the locker room.

If he'd bothered to look back at the peg, upon which the bag was now hanging, he would have seen them both disappear in a puff of purple smoke, leaving, in their place, a thin trickle of green slime, which spread across the wall, and clearly shaped itself into seven neat letters. The message read: *Goodbye*.

The next day, Terry's name tags had completely vanished. All except one – "Thief". That remained stuck fast to the back of his neck. After several hot baths, however, even the "thief" label started to fade, until, eventually it just curled up and dropped off onto his pillow one night.

Terry never stole again. He had the odd lapse, when he looked at a chocolate bar in a sweet shop, or passed an unpadlocked bicycle in the street, but it only ever took the tiniest itch on the back of his neck to pull him round to his senses.

The Locked Door

There is a room in a house, in a town, in a far away country, that no one dares enter. The door has been locked for seventy five years and in that time no living soul has set foot inside. The sign on the door reads quite simply: *BEWARE OF THE GHOST*.

Every night as the town clock strikes twelve, the most spine chilling scream heralds the start of a ritual that turns the bravest of men into quivering jellyfish. Many have tried to spend the night alone in this house, but few have lived to tell of its secret. Too often, come daybreak, their corpses are found, stiff with fear, by the window or the front door, through which they had been trying to escape.

So what is it about this haunting that makes it so terrifying? Is it the heavy hobnail boots that pace up and down the wooden floorboards all night? Is it the constant wailing and chattering that float through the house and penetrate your sleep? Is it the cries for help, or the rattling doors? Or, perhaps, it's the tiny trickle of blood that seeps through the ceiling and drips off the lightbulb in the bedroom. I think it's the rhythmical sound of the axe, chopping wood, but then I lost my thumb in a bizarre chainsaw accident, so I would, wouldn't I? Others say that the noise of the ghost hurling objects around the room would be enough to drive them mad. The truth is that behind that locked door at the top of that house, in that town, in that far away country, there are noises to terrify everyone. Except perhaps a child, a small innocent child, too young to understand what lies behind the noises that she is hearing.

Matt and Jodie came from New Zealand. They had not been married long, but they needed somewhere to live, and as they did not have much money they were forced to look at cheap houses. Of course, there was no house cheaper in the whole wide world than the one with the locked door. So they bought it. And they lived there happily for three years, strangely undisturbed by the noises that came from the locked room. Matt and Jodie were both deaf, you see. They could not hear the ghost.

After three years they had a baby daughter, and they called her Rosie, because that was the colour of her cheeks. She had a smile for everyone and would crawl around the house gurgling happily whenever her parents looked at her. Everything seemed perfect. A happy child, two loving parents and a beautiful house. And the ghost, of course. Don't forget the ghost!

Now that it knew there were people living in the house, the ghost's nightly antics got worse. Windows were smashed, floorboards were ripped up and the chilling sound of its mournful caterwauling echoed into every corner of the house. But only Rosie heard it. If Matt and Jodie had seen the tiny drops of blood which dripped from the ceiling onto Rosie's bedroom floor, I daresay they would have packed their bags and sold the house instantly, but the blood was never there in the morning. It had run down between a gap in the old floorboards and vanished from sight.

It was not surprising, therefore, that Rosie's parents were unconcerned by the ghost's conduct, until, that is, the day that Rosie went missing. They ran through the house searching everywhere. The larder, the broom cupboard, the coal hole and even the cellar, which was dark and damp and hung with cobwebs. Nothing. There was not a sign of her anywhere. Unless . . .

Matt took the stairs three at a time. He had been up to the top of the house only once, when they had first moved in, and now he could barely remember what it looked like. He and Jodie had taken one look at the sign on the locked door and decided that if they didn't disturb the ghost, then the ghost would not disturb them. But Rosie couldn't read, and she wouldn't know what the words "Beware of the Ghost" meant, even if she could. What if she had found the key and let herself in? Matt was thinking irrationally now. For the first time, he was scared of the house and the terrible secrets that it so jealously guarded.

He threw his shoulder against the locked door shouting Rosie's name for all he was worth. A pair of hobnail boots stirred on the other side of the door and scraped across the floorboards, but Matt was not aware of them. A tiny, quivering voice pleaded with Matt to open the door, but

29

Matt could not hear it. Then the door handle rattled as something tried to get out of the room. Matt *saw* that. He took one step backwards. Rosie *was* in the room. She was trying to escape. Matt charged the door for a second time, but a wall of metal bars suddenly clattered down from above his head and blocked his way. The loft ladder had mysteriously slipped out of its clip and now stood between him and the locked door. Matt froze with fear. The ghost was trying to stop him from rescuing his daughter. Matt could not let that happen. Slowly he raised his eyes, terrified by the prospect of seeing the ghost in the loft.

"Dada," said Rosie, looking down on her father. "Rosie find big hole in sky!"

From that day on, the loft was strictly out of bounds to Rosie. In fact the top floor became a bit of a no-go area for the whole family. Matt did not want to go through all that worry again, and Jodie was just plain scared.

They strung a rope across the top of the stairs and placed a basket of Kiwi bird feathers outside the locked door. This was meant to protect them from the evil spirit that lurked within. Jodie had been shown this magic trick by a Maori elder in New Zealand, but as the elder had been more than a little tipsy when he had shown her, and as he had also been trying to convince her that a nightly bath in fishballs and spinach kept Dracula away, she wasn't totally sure that it would work. Besides any ghost that had hung around for seventy five years was not just going to suddenly disappear overnight.

And nor *did* it.

Rosie stopped sleeping. The piercing cries and moans from the room above wormed their way into her dreams and turned them into nightmares. Fluffy white bunnies hopping peacefully through a sunlit meadow would suddenly find themselves devoured by the sixty foot jaws of a slavering wolf. Bags of sweets would turn into bags of black beetles and, worst of all, Rosie lost the ability to fly in her dreams. Yet strangely her fascination with the locked door never dwindled. The more Rosie heard the ghost's plaintive voice in her dreams, the more she wanted to know about it.

A while passed before Rosie got the opportunity to explore the top floor of the house again. It was the middle of the night. The town clock had just struck twelve, when Rosie was wakened by a persistent scratching noise. The sort rats make when they are trapped in a coffin. It sounded as if it was coming from the chimney. She climbed out of bed and went across to the fireplace. She could hear the scratching quite clearly now. Suddenly a cloud of dust exploded into the room and settled in Rosie's hair. The ghost was coming down the chimney!

Rosie rushed to the door and shouted. "Help! The ghost is coming to get me!"

But, of course, nobody heard her. Well, nobody living, that is.

As Rosie's cry rang out through the house, it was the ghost who answered.

"Help *me*!" said the far away voice. "Help *me*!"

It had always struck Rosie that the ghost's voice sounded rather sad and lonely. It hadn't occurred to her that this is what the ghost might want her to think, so that she would unlock the door.

"Help *me*!" came the voice again, and Rosie found herself climbing the stairs towards the locked door.

She was tall enough now to climb over the rope that stretched across the top of the stairs, and the basket of shrivelled Kiwi bird feathers was light enough for her to move it to one side. She edged closer to the door and put her ear next to it. The hobnail boots stopped pacing and turned to face the door. There was a long pause. Rosie held her breath.

"Hello," she said, in a voice so tiny that she could hardly hear it herself.

An axe thudded into a block of wood. Then there was silence. Then there was shuffling. Then there was silence again.

"Hello," said Rosie, slightly louder this time.

A thin white finger crept out from underneath the door and touched the end of Rosie's foot. She jumped back and couldn't help but scream. When she dared to look again, the finger was still there. It beckoned her forward with slow, painful movements, while the voice from behind the door whispered, "Rosie, Rosie, Rosie. Open the door!"

Then the finger disappeared.

Rosie knelt down to see if she could see anything under the door, but before she could get close enough to take a proper look, the finger was back, only this time with a key.

"Take the key, Rosie," whispered the voice. "Open the

33

door! Release me, Rosie. Take the key and open the door! Set me free, Rosie!"

Rosie was in a trance, it was as if she *had* to find out what was behind that locked door, no matter what the cost. She took the key, she put it in the lock, and her little heart raced as she turned it.

The lock had not been opened for seventy five years and was very stiff, but eventually, after a fierce struggle, she heard it click. Her tiny hand shook as she reached up to the door handle. She turned it once and entered the room that for so long had been shut off from the living world.

The room was dark and lit only by a guttering fire in the corner. Rosie could see an axe, a pile of smashed up furniture and a stack of old tins, but she could not see the ghost. Then something stirred behind her.

Rosie spun round, expecting to see a ten foot demon with bloodless eyes and a knife and fork dashing towards her, but instead, she came face to face with a shrunken, crinkly old man, with a long white beard that touched the floor.

"Well, flip me over with a candlestick," he said. Am I glad to see you! I've been waiting for someone to open that door for seventy five years! When I catch the person who locked me in here, there's going to be all hell to pay!"

"Excuse me," said Rosie, who was not as frightened of this ghost as she thought she was going to be, "are you a ghost?"

"Good heavens, no, young lady," replied the old man, "I certainly hope not. Now do you think we could go down to the kitchen and find something to eat. I am absolutely famished!"

So Rosie took the old man downstairs to meet her parents. Imagine Matt and Jodie's surprise when they discovered that there had been an old man living behind that locked door all the time, and that they had been too frightened to let him out. Imagine their surprise as well, when they realised that they could hear every single word he said.

"But Rosie told us you made such a terrifying noise," said Jodie.

"Well wouldn't you after seventy five years. It was getting to the point where I thought I was never going to be rescued," said the old man, indignantly.

"And the axe?" added Matt.

"I had to make firewood somehow, didn't I?" said the old man.

"But the drops of blood, which dripped from my ceiling," asked Rosie. "Where did they come from?"

"Ah, yes, well . . . I didn't say I was very good at using

35

the axe. I kept cutting my finger."

The old man looked embarrassed so they didn't question him further. They let him eat his slice of chocolate sponge cake instead.

As the old man picked the last cake crumb from out of his beard, and licked his boney fingers, Rosie tugged his sleeve. She had been thinking hard for sometime.

"So, how old are you?" she said.

"I'm not sure," replied the old man. "About one hundred and fifteen."

"Wow!" said Rosie. "I've never sat on anyone's lap who was that old before!"

And she leapt up to sit on the old man's lap; Instead she found herself sitting on an empty chair.

There was no old man.

A Tangled Web

Nigel could sometimes be charming. Usually when he wanted something, like a pencil with a rubber on top from Madame Tussaud's, or the last jam doughnut. Generally though, he was pretty annoying. What with those funny little clicking noises he made with his tongue, those eyeball rolls he did, when he would scare grown ups by showing them the whites of his eyes, and that terrible habit he had of standing in the middle of the room and staring at someone with his mouth wide open.

"You look like a post box!" his mother would say.

Nigel would reply by clicking his tongue.

"If the wind changes, your face will get stuck!" she'd add.

Nigel would reply by rolling the whites of his eyes.

"Oh please stop catching flies, Nigel!" his mother would say in complete exasperation.

And Nigel would reply, "But I'm a spider!"

Nigel had an unnatural passion for spiders. I don't

mean that he collected them, as some children collect stamps or marbles, because he didn't. He liked to torture them. To catch them in jam jars and pull their legs off with his mother's eyebrow tweezers. To shut them inside matchboxes and push a hundred pins through the outside until the spiders were as dead as it is spiderly possible to be. To press them in between the pages of large books like wild flowers, and, of course, to drown them in the bath and watch them flounder helplessly as the soapy whirlpool sucked them down into the dark, damp hell known to us all as "the plughole".

Not a pleasant boy, Nigel. Not exactly a friend of the spider, either.

His mother once asked him why he was so cruel to spiders if he was supposed to be a spider himself. Nigel clicked his tongue.

"There are spiders and *spiders*!" he replied cryptically. "I am the spider they all fear. I am the head spider."

"A sort of tarantula with a machine gun?" said his mother, who was trying awfully hard to understand her son.

"My name is Black Nigel!" shouted Nigel. All the spiders who were close enough to hear, scurried back into their secret places and curled up tight to stop their knees from knocking. "And Black Nigel eats spiders for breakfast!"

Nigel's mother left her son staring out of the window with his mouth open.

"He is a peculiar child," she said to Nigel's father.

"I don't know where he gets it from," said Nigel's father, sprinkling the wings of a dozen house flies over his cereal. "Still, at least the boy's got an interest. That's more than can be said for other lads of his age."

Nigel's mouth was still ajar some two hours later, when Ariadne slipped into his room between a loose floorboard and a piece of brown linoleum. Nigel was waiting to catch a fly. Ariadne was looking for somewhere warm and dry to spin a web, somewhere where she could lie down and have her babies in peace. Although she didn't know it, Ariadne could not have chosen a more dangerous spot.

Nigel's nose twitched as she ran along the skirting board and scampered up the leg of his wardrobe. His eyes rolled down to reveal their cold blue pupils and he turned his head slowly in Ariadne's direction. Just as a lizard might suck in breath prior to pouncing on a defenceless butterfly, so Nigel's mouth closed momentarily. He swallowed, licked his lips and tiptoed over to his bed, where he kept a supply of jam jars stashed away under his pillow. Fly catching forgotten, the spider hunt was on.

Ariadne, meanwhile, had spun her web and was resting after her tiring work. Her stomach was swollen with hundreds of tiny baby spiders, who kicked and shoved inside her to make themselves comfortable. It would not be long now before she gave birth, and try as she might to stay awake she was unable to stop her eyes from closing. She fell into a deep sleep and dreamt of babygrows with eight legs, and a washing line hung with a thousand wet nappies.

Ariadne's web shook as Nigel tilted the wardrobe against the wall. He knelt down and put the jar on the floor next to him. Then he took out a torch and flashed it into the dark wooden corners underneath the wardrobe, which he knew from experience were where spiders liked to hide.

Ariadne was woken by a bright searchlight shining directly into her eyes. It confused her. She couldn't see what was happening. She couldn't remember where she was. She couldn't imagine what this light was for. All she knew was that there was danger, and she had to escape to save her unborn children.

Nigel saw the spider move. It was a big one! A huge, wobbling belly that scraped along the ground as it tried to run. He yelped with delight at his catch. He held his jam jar tantalisingly over the retreating spider's head, allowed it to think that it was getting away, and then, at the very last moment, brought it crashing down. She was trapped.

"Let me out! Please let me out!" squealed Ariadne, but Nigel didn't understand Spiderspeak. Not that he would have listened even if he had.

He slipped a piece of paper over the opening to the jar, turned the jar the right way up, and laughed as Ariadne fell painfully onto her back.

"I expect you're cold," he said, clicking his tongue.

Ariadne shook her head.

"I expect you want warming up," he said rolling his eyes back.

Ariadne stood on her back legs and tried to get as close to Nigel's ear as she could.

"Kill me if you must, but don't harm my babies," she begged, but her pleas fell on deaf ears. Nigel had already lit the candle. He held it underneath the jar and moved it round and round in a circle. The glass under Ariadne's feet started to warm up. She moved to a cooler spot, but the flame followed her.

"Ow!" she screamed. "You're burning my feet!"

She tried to climb up the side of the jar, but it was too slippery. "Please stop!" she cried.

Nigel watched, impassively, as the spider with the fat belly slid back down the sides of the jar and fried.

He took the dead spider out of the jar, opened his window and dropped it into the dustbin below. Then he blew out the candle, returned the jam jar to its rightful place under his pillow, sat on his bed and sniggered.

The dustmen came the following morning. They threw Ariadne's body into the middle of a churning mass of rotting debris and drove her off to the Corporation Dump. The seagulls screeched overhead as the dustcart tipped its foul smelling cargo onto the rubbish heap, and Ariadne came to rest sandwiched between a cardboard box and a maggot infested peach.

"Nigel, please close your mouth," said his mother at dinner that night.

"And stop rolling your eyes," added his father. "How many times do we have to tell you? If the wind changes . . ."

"My face will stick, yes, I know," said Nigel, lippily. "I can't help it."

"That's because you've been doing it for so long, you've forgotten how to look normal," chided his mother.

They ate in silence. Nigel was trying to remember what his normal face looked like.

Nigel spoke first. "Can I watch the telly before bed?" he asked.

"If you promise not to pull any more faces," replied his mother.

"I promise," said Nigel, closing his mouth quickly, before his parents noticed that it had started to drift open again.

"Thanks," he said. Then, "Sorry!" as his tongue clicked of its own accord.

As darkness fell on the rubbish tip, something stirred underneath a cardboard box. A maggot infested peach rolled to one side. A dead spider turned over in its putrid grave. Ariadne had not come back to life, although if you had seen the wild bumping and thumping in her stomach you might have been forgiven for thinking that she had. The baby spiders, which she had been carrying while Nigel had so cruelly killed her, were being born. Suddenly

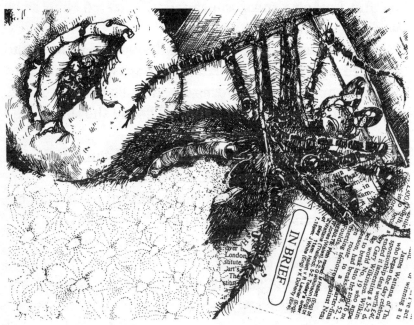

thousands upon thousands of tiny spiders burst out of her belly and floated on gossamer threads to the top of the rubbish heap. Thousands upon thousands of pale white spiders lined up along the edge of an old, rusty tin bath. They were not flesh and blood like you and me, for they too had died inside that terrible jam jar. They were a ghostly army, forty thousand legs strong, waiting for the wind to carry them off to Nigel's house.

Nigel sat in front of the telly with his bottom jaw on his chest. His mouth was open so wide you could have driven a train through it.

"Go to bed!" said his mother suddenly.

"What?" said Nigel.

"I warned you," she said, grabbing him by his arm. "Any more faces and off to bed."

"But I didn't know I was doing it!" bleated Nigel as he was hurried out of the room.

"Good!" said his mother, who was getting a tad steamed up, "Then you can go upstairs and not know you're catching flies up there!" And she slammed the sitting room door so hard that the house shook.

"You'll only have yourself to blame if the wind changes!" came the distant voice of Nigel's father.

"Oh shut up," thought Nigel, as he climbed the stairs to bed all by himself.

Outside, the wind changed direction. The ghostly spiders were lifted from their perch and blown gently across the rooftops towards Nigel's bedroom window.

Nigel was asleep when his mother went up to check on him. As usual his mouth was wide open and he was snoring thunderously. It was a bit stuffy so she opened the window, kissed him on the cheek and went off to bed herself.

She didn't see the thousands upon thousands of pale, white spiders, dripping from the branches of the apple blossom tree that stood directly beneath Nigel's window. If she had, perhaps she would never have opened it, because as she left the room the wind picked up again. It lifted the spiders out of the tree and guided them through the window. It nudged them across the room towards the bed, and it dropped them, one by one, into that gaping, snoring hole in the middle of Nigel's face.

The spiders spent a busy night in Nigel's chest. Although uninvited, they quickly made themselves at home, by spinning their delicate webs around his ribs. Come morning, they were all fast asleep, exhausted from their night's labours.

When Nigel awoke he felt very strange. His chest was tight, as if he had a bad cold, and it hurt him when he breathed. He coughed to clear his throat. A tiny spider popped out of his mouth and scuttled away into the folds of his duvet. Nigel looked at the ceiling. There were no spiders up there, so where had it come from? He coughed again. Another spider popped onto his bed. Nigel shut his mouth. He could feel something crawling around in his throat. Surely not? He coughed for a third time just to check and let out a feeble scream. The spiders *were* coming out of his mouth!

At breakfast that morning, Nigel's parents noticed that

he kept his mouth firmly closed.

"Learnt your lesson?" said his mother smugly.

"Yes. Definitely," mumbled Nigel, between pursed lips. "I'll never open my mouth again!"

And he never did. From that day onwards Nigel kept his mouth shut tight, for fear that another spider might pop out. He stopped rolling his eyes and clicking his tongue as well.

He took up knitting instead. He would sit all alone, for hours on end, winding lengths of white wool between the bedposts at either end of his bed. He had no idea why he did it. He just knew that he had to. It was instinctive.

Just like a spider spinning its web.

The Well

Granny and Grandpa Halley lived in a beautiful cottage in Devon, called "Wellsdeep". Granny Halley spent most of her days in the garden, tending the flowerbeds and picking the raspberries and blackcurrants that grew in abundance up the wall behind the compost heap. Grandpa Halley had bought himself a garden buggy. He would spend his days driving around trimming the lawn, and stopping occasionally to do battle with an enormous weed.

In the centre of the garden there was an old well, from which the cottage's name had derived. According to Parish records the well had been there for over eleven hundred years. If you dropped a stone in at the top, it would fall for twenty six seconds before it hit the water. The well was very deep. Over one hundred and forty feet, to be precise.

Granny and Grandpa Halley had two grandchildren. Louis and Ben. Ben was the oldest, but not by much. They were not particularly naughty children, but they did like sticking their fingers into things that ought not to have little fingers stuck in them. Let's face it, they were ordinary kids. Inquisitive, clumsy, obstinate and above all, fearlessly attracted to water. Like mice to a mousetrap.

Granny Halley pushed the sun hat off her eyes and rested her hands on her broad, aching hips.

"Cooeee!" she shouted, "Grandpa!"

Grandpa Halley chugged up on his buggy.

"Yes m'dear," he said, knocking the tobacco out of his pipe onto her begonias.

"I do wish you wouldn't do that, John," she said.

"Sorry, old dear. What did you want me for?"

"The well," said Granny Halley. "The grandchildren arrive tomorrow and you have promised to block it up."

"Have I?" said Grandpa Halley.

"You know you have," said his wife. "Now run along and do it. We don't want Louis and Ben falling down the well on their first morning, now do we?"

"Couldn't it wait?"

"No," said Granny Halley, emphatically.

"I'll tell you what I'll do," said Grandpa Halley, putting on his 'I am thinking deeply' face. "First thing tomorrow morning, I'll go down to the shops and buy a plank of wood and some nails. I'll have the whole thing finished by lunchtime."

"It would be simpler if you just did it now," insisted Granny Halley.

"Not tonight, dear. I haven't finished the mowing. Tomorrow morning's best."

"Very well," said his wife, picking up her trowel. "If

you promise."

"That's the spirit," said Grandpa Halley as he pootled off again on his buggy. "Tomorrow morning, you'll see."

The next morning Grandpa Halley had a lie in. Once he had finished his breakfast in bed, consisting of three boiled eggs, a jug of orange juice, several cups of black coffee and a plate of marmite soldiers, it was time for his bath. A ritual, hour-long soak, listening to Gardener's Question Time on Radio Four. Then he shaved, brushed his hair, straightened his tie and went downstairs. It was twelve fifteen.

Granny Halley was waiting for him. Her lips were ever so slightly pinched, and she was affecting an air of general business, although she actually had nothing to do.

"And what about the well?" she said, brusquely.

Grandpa Halley looked surprised. "The well?"

"The well," she repeated, "which you were going to board up this morning."

"Good heavens no, old dear. I said I'd do that this afternoon."

"No you didn't," said his wife.

"Didn't I?" said Grandpa Halley, innocently.

"This afternoon," she continued, "the children arrive. There will not be time to do it this afternoon."

"What a shame," he said. "Well, I'll just have to do it tomorrow morning," and off he went to sharpen the blades on his rotor mower.

Louis and Ben arrived at three o'clock with their parents. At five past three, their parents left. They were late, and had just two hours to catch their plane to Venice.

The children stood in the hall clutching their suitcases.

"Well," said Granny Halley, "isn't this nice. Let's go and see Grandpa in the garden."

Grandpa was asleep in his potting shed. He was trying to sneak forty winks while his wife wasn't watching.

"Hello, Grandpa," said Ben.

Grandpa woke with a start, and upset the bottle of beer which he had hidden in his jumper.

"Good heavens, there you are. I've been waiting out here for hours for you two to arrive."

"You were asleep," said Louis.

"No, no, no," he snorted, "just giving my eyelids a rest. Now come along, let's go and explore."

Granny Halley put her hand up to stop them. "One thing before you go, children," she said, "don't go near the well. Your grandfather will be boarding it up tomorrow morning, but in the meantime it's not safe. Do you understand?"

Louis and Ben nodded seriously. Then Granny Halley left to worry about dinner.

That night Grandpa Halley couldn't sleep. Everytime he tried to snuggle down, something tickled his feet. Everytime he tried to close his eyes a little hand tugged them open again. Then he heard laughter. Childish laughter coming from underneath his bed. He thought it was his grandchildren, but when he took a look under the bed there was nothing there. Except the potty, of course.

"How very strange," he thought to himself. "Good Lord, there it is again!"

The laughter was more distant now. It was coming from outside in the garden. He crawled out of bed and went over to the window. The curtain was slightly open, and through the gap he could see the well. Unless his old ears were playing tricks on him, it was the well that was laughing. The well was laughing at him!

"Just because I haven't had time to board you over," thought Grandpa Halley, crossly. He shook his fist at the well and shouted, "I'll show you! Tomorrow morning, you'll see!"

Granny Halley sat up in bed and got quite a shock.

"What on earth do you think you're doing, John?"

"Just having a couple of words with the well, dear," said an embarrassed Grandpa Halley.

"Well come back to bed," scolded his wife. "You look ridiculous!" Which he did. "You do *know* you've forgotten to put your pyjamas on, don't you?"

Grandpa Halley looked down and sprang back into bed like a naked gazelle.

Tomorrow morning arrived. At nine o'clock precisely, Grandpa Halley marched out of his potting shed carrying a tape measure, a pencil and the look of an extremely busy man. He reached the well at nine o'two, and proceeded to walk around it several times, stroking his chin and shaking his head wisely. Then he unwound his tape measure and laid it across the opening to the well. As he bent down to read it, the measure rolled up, back flipped off the edge of the well and disappeared into the water one hundred and forty feet below. Grandpa Halley stood absolutely still. Then he screamed with rage, tore off his hat and hurled it down the well after the tape measure. Louis and Ben watched this from their bedroom window

51

and decided that he had just gone mad.

"It can't be done!" said Grandpa Halley to his wife. "Not until tomorrow, at least. This job needs specialist equipment. You know, hammer, saw . . ." He couldn't think of anything else. "I need more time to plan."

"Yes dear," replied Granny Halley, who knew from experience that there was no point in arguing with him when he was in this kind of mood. Even though she knew he was wrong.

After lunch Grandpa Halley had a sleep, well-earned in his opinion, while Granny Halley dead-headed a few roses. Louis and Ben were playing hide and seek by the raspberry canes, when Louis spotted a wooden bucket.

"Let's play pirates!" he yelled, running across the lawn and jumping inside it. "I'm look out."

"And I be Long John Silver," said Ben, closing one eye and hopping around on his left leg.

"Land ahoy!" bellowed Louis, rocking backwards and forwards in the bucket, as if caught in the eye of a fierce storm. He was getting quite carried away in his crow's nest. He grabbed the rope that was hanging by his side and threw it to Ben.

"Ha ha! Heave ho, me hearty matey!" he ordered.

"Righto, Captain," said Ben, taking the rope and giving it a tug. The bucket slid across the lawn, and lifted off the ground. Louis squealed with both terror and delight. He was flying!

Granny Halley dabbed her hot head with a handkerchief. She heard the boys' shrieks of uncontrolled excitement, and glanced across at them. Her heart stopped. The hairs on the back of her neck stood up. Her fingertips turned icy cold.

"Benjamin!" she shouted. She was up and running. "Benjamin! Stop!"

Louis was not in a crow's nest. He was sitting in the water bucket. The water bucket was attached to the rope, which Benjamin was holding, and the rope ran through a shiney, black pulley which was bolted onto a block of wood, right over the centre of the well.

Louis was pointing out to sea, unaware of the one hundred and forty foot drop into the water beneath him. Ben was pretending to see land too. He let go of the rope to shade his eyes. Louis screamed as the bucket slipped downwards and then, suddenly, jammed to a halt again. Granny Halley sat on the lawn, crying. The rope held firmly between her two shaking hands.

Grandpa Halley was woken with a bucket of cold water in his face.

"You lazy, good-for-nothing old bag of bones," she ranted. "They could have been killed. Stop putting off till tomorrow what you should be doing today. Find some wood and fix the well!"

"Point taken," said Grandpa, looking at his wife's ashen face. "Tomorrow morning. I'll be there. Just you see if I'm not." Then he lay back down, closed his eyes and dreamed of a thousand new excuses for not blocking up the well.

There was a full moon that night. Once again, Grandpa Halley could not sleep. Once again, he was prodded from his slumbers by little tickling fingers. Once again, he heard the distant, childish laughter, which floated up from the well and crept into his bedroom through the open window. He got up to investigate.

The well was bathed in an eerie half-light, and stood glowing in the middle of the garden. At first this was all Grandpa Halley could see, but, gradually, as his eyes adjusted, he could make out a tiny figure emerging from the back of the cottage, and running across the lawn. He rubbed his eyes, thinking that the light was playing a trick on them, but the figure did not disappear. Its image grew stronger, until Grandpa Halley was convinced that he could see, standing on the edge of the well, a small child.

"Benjamin?" whispered Grandpa Halley. "Louis?"

The child held out his hand to Grandpa Halley, then toppled backwards and, silently, fell in.

Grandpa Halley dashed down the stairs and ran outside to the well, expecting to find a boy. There was none. He flashed a torch down into the dark depths, but

all he could see was the glinting water. He leant out over the black hole and called out, but only *his* voice replied. Then he heard a laugh behind him and felt a tiny hand press into the small of his back. Before he could turn round, he had lost his balance. He scraped his face as he fell. He pushed his arms and legs against the brick walls, but he could not stop himself from sliding one hundred and forty feet into the cold, slimy water below.

The shock of hitting the water brought him round. He shouted for help as his hands fumbled to gain a hold on the shiny walls. Fortunately there was a ledge just above his head and he managed to pull himself up to safety. He spat out a mouthful of brackish water and called out again.

"I'll help," said a small voice underneath the water.

Grandpa Halley's eyes nearly dropped out of their sockets as a small boy, with a face like a blueberry, rose up out of the water and settled down on the ledge next to him.

"You should have nailed some wood over the top," he said.

"Who are you?" said Grandpa Halley.

"I am the Ghost of Jobs Left Undone," said the boy.

"The Ghost of what?" spluttered Grandpa Halley.

"Jobs Left Undone," repeated the boy. "If you had blocked in this well when you were meant to, none of this would have ever happened."

"But I was going to do it tomorrow."

"That's what my Grandfather kept saying," said the boy, "but he never did. That's why I fell to my death down this well."

"Grandpa!" Two little voices bounced down the walls.

56

Grandpa Halley looked up. He could just make out the dressing-gowned figures of Louis and Ben, leaning over the top of the well.

"We've come to save you," announced Ben. "We heard you shouting!"

"Stay where you are," replied Grandpa. "On no account move. It's too dangerous."

"It's all right," responded Louis, cheerfully, "we know what to do."

Then Louis and Ben got into the bucket, held on to the rope, and slowly inched their way into the well.

"No," roared Grandpa. "The rope won't take the weight!"

But he was too late. The rope snapped and Louis and Ben fell like rocks towards the water.

"No," shouted Grandpa, sitting up in bed.

"What is it?" said Granny Halley.

"Nothing," he lied. "Just a dream."

Then he lay down in his soaking wet pyjamas and tried to get back to sleep.

The next day, the well was boarded up before Louis and Ben had even got out of bed. Grandpa Halley was taking no more chances.

"Well done," said Granny Halley, admiring his clumsy handiwork. "And about time too."

Grandpa Halley looked sheepish and picked a nail out from in between his teeth.

"Well, now that you've done that job," she added, "you can paint the outside of the house. You've been meaning to do that for ages."

"Tomorrow," said Grandpa Halley. "I'll do it tomorrow!"

An Elephant Never Forgets

If you know what happened to Belinda and Percy Crumpdump then don't say a word, because you'll only spoil the ending for the others. If you've never heard of them, then I must warn you now that the story you are about to hear is full of greed, misfortune, sadness, cruelty and just desserts. Those of a nervous disposition should close the book right now.

So, you've decided to stay, have you? Very brave.

Belinda and Percy Crumpdump belonged to Mr and Mrs Crumpdump of Crumpdump Road, Crumpdump Town, in Crumpdump County. Mr Crumpdump was a very, very wealthy man and owned an entire town all by himself. Mrs Crumpdump was no pauper either. She had made her fortune by waiting for her father to die, which she had done with little grace and much impatience. They were not the most pleasant family in the world, and just as the old saying says, money was not able to buy them happiness.

58

It did buy them a safari holiday in Africa, though.

They drove through the African bush in their open-top Rolls Royce looking at the wildlife. Their guide was a friendly old man called Roger, who had lived in Africa all his life and knew everything there was to know about wild animals. He knew where they slept, where they played, where they ate their lunch and most importantly where they went to get away from the prying eyes of families like the Crumpdumps. This is why Mr Crumpdump had hired Roger, because he wanted his family to see the animals that nobody else had ever seen before. Animals truly in the wild.

Roger certainly knew his stuff. He spent day after hot day running in front of the Rolls Royce, looking for signs that would tell him whether there were any animals about. He found plenty. The Crumpdumps saw a sleepy tiger stretched out on a high branch, next to an impala that he had just killed and dragged up the tree for his breakfast. They saw a flange of baboons grooming each other by the edge of a lake, a herd of giraffes moving gracefully across an open plain, thousands of wildebeest, a family of lions, and a funny looking pig called a warthog.

Yet Belinda and Percy never once showed even the tiniest flicker of interest.

"I want to see an elephant," moaned Belinda.

"If we'd wanted to see lions," added a very grumpy Percy, "we could have popped along to London Zoo!"

Mr Crumpdump stopped the car. Mrs Crumpdump was crying.

"What is it, dear?" he said, offering her a towel to wipe her eyes with.

"Our little babies are not happy!" blubbed the stupid woman in the bush hat.

Mr Crumpdump stood up in the car and shouted for Roger.

"Yes sir," said Roger, when he arrived seconds later, panting.

"Call yourself a guide!" sneered Mr Crumpdump. "My children want to see an elephant, and you haven't managed to produce one yet!"

"I'm doing my best, sir," said Roger, "but elephants do not grow on trees."

"More's the pity!" sniped Percy. "We might see one if they did!"

Luckily for Roger, it was not long before they did see some elephants. In fact they very nearly ran them over. A large family crossed the road in front of the Rolls Royce as it turned the next corner. The bull elephant lead the way, followed by six young ones. They had their trunks wrapped around each others' tails so as not to get lost. Bringing up the rear was the mother. She was very nervous and trumpeted loudly when she saw the car, for fear that the Crumpdumps might attack her brood.

"Aren't they just gorgeous," said Belinda.

"I want one," said Percy.

Mrs Crumpdump was quick to reply. "I am not having an elephant in my house," she said.

"Meany!" said Percy. "You never let us have what we want! Why not?"

"Because I don't want them pooping on my new carpet," said Mrs Crumpdump.

Belinda tossed the curls off her forehead and laughed at

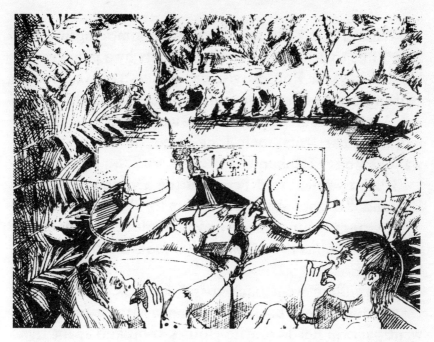

her mother. "Oh, Mummy!" she said. "You are a silly mummy! It wouldn't have to be alive."

"No, we could shoot it," added Percy.

"A dead elephant!" said their horrified mother. "It would smell the house down. No! And that's my final word."

Belinda went all gooey and stroked her father's hair. She knew every trick in the book when it came to getting what she wanted.

"Pleeeeeease, Daddy," she said in her most sugary voice. "Pretty please with pink bows on!"

"We'll see," said Mr Crumpdump, beaming munificently.

"But you are not allowed to kill elephants," said Roger who had been listening to every word. "It is against the law."

"WE WILL SEE!" said Mr Crumpdump angrily. He didn't like to be contradicted, especially by a paid guide. He slammed the Rolls Royce into gear and drove off in a swirling cloud of dust, squashing Roger's foot as he went.

Belinda and Percy sulked all the way home. They made it quite clear from their long-faced silence that they wanted a baby elephant.

"It's only one," said Percy on the aeroplane back to England. "It's not as if we're asking for the whole herd."

Mr Crumpdump smiled a private smile behind his copy of *Money Makers' Monthly*, and took another sip of brandy.

The children went back to school a week later. Mr Crumpdump went back to work and Mrs Crumpdump went back to her favourite clothes shop and spent five thousand pounds on a dress that she wasn't sure she'd ever wear.

One morning, while the Portuguese maid was spreading caviar on Belinda's toast, the doorbell rang.

"I'll get it!" shouted Percy, leaping up from the table before anyone could stop him.

It was the postman, carrying a huge parcel wrapped up in brown paper and string.

"Master Percy Crumpdump?" said the postman.

"Yes," said Percy.

"Got a parcel here for you and your sister. Hot foot from Africa, you might say!" He chuckled at his own joke, but Percy didn't understand it.

"Who is it?" shouted Mr Crumpdump, from the bathroom upstairs.

"The postman with a hot foot from Africa," Percy shouted back.

Mr Crumpdump bounded down the stairs in his dressing gown, his face still covered with shaving foam, and said, "Oh good! I thought it would never arrive."

Then he gave the startled postman a £50 note, shut the front door, and carefully carried the parcel into the sitting room.

By now Belinda had joined them, all thoughts of Beluga Toast banished from her mind.

"What is it?" she said excitedly, jumping up and down on her mother's new carpet.

"Why don't you open it and see," said Mr Crumpdump. His grin now stretched from ear to ear and there was a very real possibility that if it grew much wider his face might split in two.

The children tore at the brown paper and string until their fingers bled. Thirty seconds later they had uncovered their father's secret. It was grey, it was about four feet tall, and it had five white toenails.

"Oh," said Percy.

"What is it?" said Belinda.

"It's disgusting!" said Mrs Crumpdump, who had just walked in.

"It's an elephant's foot," said Mr Crumpdump, proudly.

"Yes, but what is it?" said Belinda, again.

"It's an elephant's foot umbrella stand."

The children smiled weakly at their father. He had definitely gone a bit soft in the head. What did *they* want with an umbrella stand?

Mr Crumpdump continued, "You remember those baby elephants we saw in Africa, the ones you wanted to bring home with you?"

They nodded.

"Well, obviously, I couldn't bring a whole elephant back to England, so I had a hunter cut off one of the baby's feet. Isn't it lovely?"

Percy looked a trifle confused. "Do you mean to say that one of those baby elephants that we saw is walking around with only three legs?" he asked.

"Of course not," said his father.

Percy and Belinda looked relieved.

"Of course he's not walking around. He's dead. I had him shot before I chopped his leg off!"

"That was kind of you," said Belinda.

There was an uneasy silence, because nobody knew what to say next. It was Mr Crumpdump who spoke first.

"Good, well I'm glad you like it. I'll put it in the hall next to the leopard skin rug!"

After the initial shock of seeing a dead elephant's foot in their sitting room, the children grew to like their new present. They were the envy of their schoolfriends, who all wanted one too. This helped to make the elephant's foot seem even more special in the eyes of Belinda and Percy. Besides they had got what they wanted, and that was the main thing.

It also proved to be most handy for storing umbrellas, especially as a spate of bad weather had just settled in over England.

It had been raining non-stop for three weeks when Mrs Crumpdump announced that she was taking the children to the shops to buy them some new shoes.

"Do we have to?" moaned goggle-eyed Percy, who was slouched on the sofa watching his fifth video in a row.

"Yes we do," said his mother, sharply.

"But we'll get soaked," whined Belinda.

"A little bit of water never did anyone any harm," said Mrs Crumpdump, holding out their red macintoshes and sou'westers. The children dragged their grumpy feet into the hall.

"I wish it would stop raining," said Belinda as she took an umbrella from the elephant's foot.

"Huh! Fat chance of that!" muttered Percy.

And the rain stopped. In less time than it takes to turn off a tap, the black thunder clouds disappeared, giving way to a clear blue African sky.

Belinda looked at Percy. Percy looked at Belinda. Then they both looked at their mother. But Mrs Crumpdump was looking in her handbag for the car keys.

"Did you see that?" shouted Belinda. "I wished that the rain would stop and it did! I can do magic!"

"No you can't," said Percy. "That was a fluke."

"No it wasn't. I'll do it again if you don't believe me!"

She looked very seriously at the sky, rolled back her eyes, and chanted in a sort of deep magician's voice, "I wish it would start raining again."

But nothing happened. If anything, the sun shone even brighter.

"Told you," teased Percy.

"But I did make it stop raining, I did!" Belinda threw a tantrum and hurled the umbrella back into the elephant's foot.

And it started raining again.

This time, Belinda and Percy did not look at each other. Their eyes were firmly fixed on the elephant's foot. The same thought flashed through their heads at exactly the same time. Percy grabbed the umbrella first and shouted, "I wish I was twenty feet tall!"

His mother screamed as suddenly he shot upwards and disappeared through the hall ceiling. His head crashed through the floorboards of the bathroom like a battering ram. Percy rubbed the egg on his huge forehead and said, "Actually, I wish I wasn't," and he shrank back to his normal size.

Belinda was frantically waiting for the umbrella, but once she had got it in her hands she couldn't think of anything to wish for.

"I wish . . . I wish . . . I wish . . . I wish I had a poster of Jason Donovan!" she screamed at last. And there it was, neatly rolled up inside the elephant's foot umbrella stand.

Mrs Crumpdump lay unconscious on the floor as Belinda and Percy hugged the magic elephant's foot. It was quite the most brilliant toy they had ever had, and they danced with glee around its five white toenails.

But magic is not a toy. Children very rarely treat their toys with respect, and, of course, *respect* is what you must have for magic. Otherwise it can turn against you. I don't think that Belinda and Percy knew this.

At first they wished for simple things like sweets and ice cream, but they quickly became bored and set their sights on bigger and more expensive acquisitions. Belinda got a pony, a pair of skis and a live-in hairdresser, while Percy concentrated more on the death and destruction range of modern toys; a complete set of Action Men, a solid gold gladiator's shield and a fully armed, electric Sherman Tank.

The trouble with Belinda and Percy was that because they had so much already, there was very little that they actually needed. As a result their wishes became more and more silly.

"I wish I didn't have to take a bath!" said Percy one night. Seconds later the hot water ran out and he went to bed dirty.

On another occasion Belinda said, "I wish I didn't have to go to school today," and the school burnt down before break.

Then one day, the inevitable happened. Belinda and Percy came to make a wish, and discovered that they had asked for everything they could possibly think of. Their bedrooms were so full of toys and books and pets that the doors wouldn't shut. They sat glumly, staring at the grey elephant's foot.

"I wish I knew what to wish for next," said Belinda.

They stared some more.

Then, slowly, an idea formed in her mind. The elephant's foot had obviously heard her wish and was granting it.

"That's brilliant!" shrieked Belinda jumping up and taking hold of the umbrella.

"What is?" said Percy.

"The wish I've just though of," replied Belinda. "Do you remember all that time ago when we first asked for an elephant?"

"What a daft question!" tutted Percy. "Of course I do."

"Well, what if we bring the elephant that Daddy had shot, back to life!"

Percy wasn't at all sure.

"We could thank him," continued Belinda, "for the use of his magic foot."

"No," said Percy. "I don't think we should. What's dead is best left dead in my opinion."

"Oh come on, baby," goaded Belinda, "it'll be fun."

"It'll be all smelly and dead," said Percy, but his common sense held no sway with his sister. She rolled back her eyes, withdrew the umbrella from the elephant's foot and intoned, "I wish that the elephant, which my daddy had killed, was still alive today, and living with us now in this house."

There was a terrible roar from the landing. A high-pitched trumpeting which told of such suffering, that it froze Belinda's blood. They saw the trunk first, sneaking round the bannisters, followed by the baby elephant itself, stumbling blindly down the first flight of stairs and crashing to the ground with a cry of innocent rage. It rolled helplessly on its back as it tried to get up, but with only three legs it had little chance.

"No!" screamed Belinda. "I meant you to have four legs!"

The baby elephant turned its sad eyes towards the two children, who, all that time ago, had called so adamantly for its death. Its leg was bleeding. It was crying from the pain.

"Send him back!" shouted Percy. "Wish for him to go away!"

But Belinda could not move a muscle.

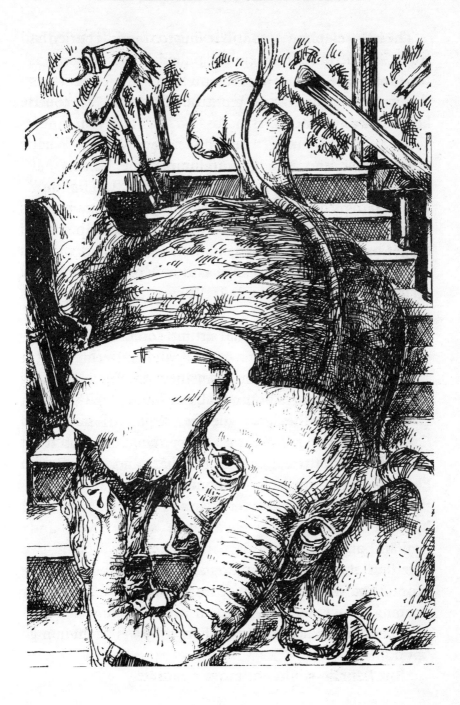

The baby elephant was still trying to stand. It curled its trunk around the bannisters and pulled, but its weight was too great. The rods collapsed and the baby elephant was thrown forward, like a huge bowling ball. It rolled helplessly down the stairs, across Mrs Crumpdump's new carpet, and straight over Belinda and Percy.

When Mr and Mrs Crumpdump came home, they found the house in a terrible mess. The stairs were smashed to pieces, the elephant's foot umbrella stand had been stolen, and worst of all Mrs Crumpdump's new carpet had bits of squashed children all over it.

"I'll never get it clean!" she said to Mr Crumpdump.

"Never mind, dear" he said. "I can always buy you a new one."

Then they went into the sitting room and poured themselves a brandy.

The baby elephant's ghost was never seen again, and yet the Crumpdump's house remains haunted to this day. Every night, in the hours before dawn, Mr and Mrs Crumpdump are woken by the piercing cries of two children. The flattened ghosts of Belinda and Percy float, like two playing cards, from room to room, searching for the baby elephant. They are trying to say sorry. But the baby elephant's ghost is never there, so they weep and wail and pull their hair out.

In fact, the ghosts of Belinda and Percy make so much noise that Mr and Mrs Crumpdump have stopped sleeping altogether now, and in a week's time they're getting divorced, which serves them jolly well right in my opinion.

School Dinners

There are some boys and girls who like school dinners. There are others who detest them.

I knew a boy once called Elgin. We used to call him Bluebottle, because he had the manners of a house fly. To say that he liked school food would not do him justice. He worshipped it. He would quite literally fall to his knees at the end of every meal and bow his head in the direction of Matron, (any other school would have called her the dinner lady, but my school liked to pretend it was posh, so it *had* to be Matron). For ages I thought he was just being polite, but when I realised that he was in fact licking everyone else's dinner droppings off the floorboards under the table, it made me feel quite sick.

"You are disgusting!" I'd shout.

Elgin's head would appear over the table top, his mouth brimming with pork fat and cauliflower leaves. "Yum, yum," he'd say. "Deeelicious!"

As if this behaviour was not enough to convince me

that human beings were still basically animals, who *just happened* to be able to drive cars, Elgin had one further trick up his grubby little sleeve. In the middle of each table was a slop bowl, into which every child would scrape the bits of their meal that they couldn't eat. The fat, the bones, the slugs, the grit and occasionally the potatoes. After he had hoovered up under the table, Elgin would grab the slop bowl, wave it about over his head and enquire if there were any takers. Then, while the rest of us closed our eyes and fought back the rising nausea in our throats, Elgin would down the contents of this bowl in one.

Afterwards he'd always burp, and always say: "Pardon me! Mustn't forget my manners."

I shared a table with Elgin for five years. Little wonder

then that over a period of time I slowly came to loathe the sight of school dinners. You cannot imagine how I suffered when Matron slapped a dollop of stewed peas, six pieces of bacon rind and a hunk of liver, still packed full of rubber tubes, onto my plate. She might as well have given me a cowpat to eat. I think I would have preferred it.

My parents got very angry with me. They told me I was stupid and selfish. That there were hungry people who'd give their right arms to eat what I chose to throw away. I would have been happy to send it to them, but Elgin had always eaten my left overs before I had a chance to wrap them up.

Sometimes, just to please my parents, I would try to look on the bright side.

"What's for pudding?" I'd say cheerfully, as Matron pumped the watery meat stew into my bowl.

"Lumpy, cold rice with sweet cherry jam," she'd reply, "or prunes!"

Was there no escaping this living hell?

The answer, sadly, was no.

I was plagued by Matron. She had got wind of the fact that I did not like my school food and used to shadow me around the dining hall. She lurked behind stacks of freezing cold hot-plates, she loitered by the serving hatch, and worst, and most embarrassing of all, she would follow me into the toilet to check that I was not spitting my food out.

"If you don't eat the food, young man," she said to me one day, as I sat staring at a plate of kedgeree, "you will sit here till it gets cold."

"But it's cold already!" I said. "That's why I can't eat it."

Her nostrils flared. "Then you will sit here until it gets even colder or until it's full of maggots, whichever is the sooner!"

"But it's full of maggots already!" I said. "That's why I can't eat it."

Her eye started to twitch. "Then you will sit here until YOU are full of maggots," she said triumphantly.

I didn't want to die in the school dining room.

"Now eat it!" she screamed. A little drop of saliva dripped from the corner of her mouth and settled, like a money spider, on my food. Then she stood over me until I had eaten every last morsel.

This sort of thing went on most days. I got into such a panic about what Matron was going to force me to eat for lunch, that I asked my parents to write me a note, saying that I was the only person in the world suffering from a rare disease called Schooldinnerphobia. This was a most unfortunate affliction which meant that if I ate school dinners I would die, instantly, and the person who was in charge of my table would immediately be sent to prison for the rest of her life, for murder. Matron always looked after our table, so I thought that she would probably get the message.

Much to my surprise, my parents sent a note to Matron, along these lines, and it seemed to have the right effect. The day I brought the note in, I was excused from eating school dinner. Matron made me eat the note instead!

I'm sure that had it not been for my unfortunate association with Elgin and Matron I would have had much the same attitude as any other child towards school dinners. As it was, though, I was seriously disturbed. I could not sleep for dreaming of huge rancid chops leaping out from behind doors, pressing me to the ground and demanding to be eaten. The smell of boiled cabbage and burnt custard returned to me with increasing frequency, and then one day, when I was twenty-two years old, I had my first flashback.

I was standing in a tightly packed lift, minding my own business and watching out for my floor, when suddenly my stomach started churning. As I tried to pretend to the onlookers in the lift that it was not *my* stomach making that awful grumbling noise, my mouth joined in. My jaws started to chomp of their own accord. My throat started salivating and the revolting stench of greasy spotted dick filled my nostrils. People were staring at me. I was chewing my tongue like a madman. I tried to smile, but whenever I did I just burped, and every time I burped, a lump of spotted dick popped, from nowhere, into my mouth. I couldn't spit it out, not in front of all those people, so, to my complete disgust, I was forced to eat it ... just as I had been forced to eat spotted dick by Matron, all those years before.

My school dinners had come back to haunt me.

From this day on, things went from bad to worse. The very sight or smell of food would trigger the most alarming responses from within my body. If someone was cooking baked beans I found myself crawling under their kitchen table and shouting: "No! No! NO! I won't come out. I HATE baked beans!"

Carrots had a similar effect *and* tomato ketchup, especially if it reeked of vinegar. I had lost control. Something had taken me over, and I was completely at its mercy.

One night, I took my girlfriend to a very posh restaurant. It was an important evening for me and I was desperate to leave her with the impression that I was a cool, laid-back guy, whom it was well worth getting to know better. The waiter took our coats and showed us to a candlelit table for two in the corner.

"Perfect," I thought, "she's going to love this."

The menu was superb. Lobster, medallions of beef, grilled sole, lamb noisettes and countless other dishes that could not have reminded me *less* of those poisonous school dinners. It was a great relief. I felt confident, for the first time in months, that I was not going to experience a psychic flashback. At the bottom of the menu there was a special notice printed in gold ink. It read:

FOR THE PERFECT NIGHT OUT, WHY NOT TRY
OUR CHEF'S SPECIALITY
ONLY £125 FOR 2 persons

How could I resist? I ordered champagne, the chef's speciality for two, and sat back to gaze deeply into my loved one's eyes.

A few minutes later, three trumpeters approached our table, stood to attention behind my chair and blew a fanfare. The other people in the restaurant stopped eating and turned to look. The Head Waiter emerged from the kitchens wheeling a trolley, with a huge gold plate on it. The restaurant applauded, my girlfriend laughed, and the Chef's Speciality was ceremoniously brought to our table.

What an evening this was turning out to be.

"With the compliments of the chef," said the Head Waiter, taking the lid off the gold plate.

My stomach lurched, my throat tightened and I could hear Matron chiding me to eat it all up, or else.

"No, I won't!" I shouted, pulling the tablecloth off the table and upsetting champagne all over my girlfriend. "You can't make me!"

"Monsieur," said the Head Waiter, who was a little alarmed. "Is it not to your liking?"

"I HATE FISH CAKES!" I wailed. "THEY MAKE ME THROW UP!"

Everyone was watching me now, but I wasn't aware of them. I was back in school. Even the Head Waiter had started to look like Matron.

"Eat it up, Monsieur," he said.

"Won't! Won't! Won't! Won't!" I said clamping my lips tightly shut.

"I shall tell your mummy how naughty you have been!" said the waiter.

"Don't care! Can't eat fish cakes!" I yelled. Then I threw a bread roll at him, and disappeared under the table.

My girlfriend had started crying by now. In fact she'd left. She had never been so embarrassed in all her life. I could see her point.

The Head Waiter was trying Matron's old trick.

"Shall we park Daddy's car in the garage?" he said holding out a spoonful of fish cake. Then he added, "Brmmm Brmmm! See what a shiny red car it is!"

I poked my head above the table to look, and he grabbed my chin, forcing my mouth open.

"Open the garage doors!" he said loudly. "Because here it comes!"

I yelled and kicked and thumped the table as he tried to force the food into my mouth. I even spat some in his face. In the end, though, I must have eaten the fishcake, because when I woke up on the pavement outside the restaurant it was all round my mouth, like a breadcrumb moustache.

This all happened many years ago. I'm an old man now. Most of my life has been spent in the shadow of this terrible haunting. I still have flashbacks if I see an advert for mashed potato or pass a cafe selling black chips, but I have found that by living alone and seeing no one, I have been able to keep the ghost of school dinners more or less at bay.

Unfortunately next week is my eighty-third birthday, and I am going to live in an Old People's Home. I won't pretend I'm happy about it, because I'm not. You see, there's a Matron there, (a very familiar-looking Matron), who has promised me that the first thing she's going to do when I arrive is start feeding me up!

The Big Sleep

A son asked his father, "Daddy," he said, "how do I know, that what is happening to me now isn't a dream?"

"Because you know that it isn't," said the father.

"No, I don't," said the son. "For all I know, what happens to me in my dreams could be the real world. My whole life could be one long sleep, and the first time I really wake up will be when I'm dead."

"Pinch yourself," said the father.

"Ow!" said the son.

"Well, there you are. You can FEEL what is happening now. A dream is something fantastic that only happens in your head."

"But what if it's the other way round. What if I'm dreaming now?"

"You're not," said the father.

"But I might be."

"No, because otherwise I'm having exactly the same dream as you," said the father.

"It's possible," said the son. "You, sitting here beside me *might* be a dream. What's to say it isn't?"

"Logic," said the father. "Dreams don't make sense. They're flights of fancy. They cannot be explained, but real life can."

"But just suppose it *was* the other way round," said the son.

"What? If life was bizarre and magical, and dreams dull and ordinary?" The father smiled. "It will never happen."

Then the father unstuck his tail from the ceiling, and fell upwards to the floor. He sang a lullaby through one of his bellybuttons, screwed in his teeth, kissed his son with eight pairs of purple lips, and switched off the light by sticking a sausage in his ear.

"Now go to sleep," said the father to his son. "Sweet dreams."

Bogman

A sharp, icy wind whistled between the six rocks that had been laid out in a rough circle. On each rock sat a man, powerfully built with broad, muscular shoulders, arms hanging like elephants' trunks below his knees, and thick matted hair clinging to his short body. Six spears lay unattended by a slab of rock in the centre of the circle, and on the slab lay the body of the victim, another man, bound hand and foot by thorny ropes. He lay silent, unmoving, while his captors decided his fate, shouting to make themselves heard in a strange language that sounded more animal than human.

A sabre-toothed tiger roared from its lair in the mountains and then fell silent.

The Stone Age Court was in session. Marg, the son of Fane, lay terrified on the cold slab of rock, knowing that if he were found guilty of stealing cattle from his brother he would surely be put to death. A thunder cloud rumbled in the black sky and spat out its first drops of rain. The eldest

83

of the captors stood up and walked towards Marg. He picked up a spear and held it high above his head. The others fell silent. Then with one almighty, blood-curdling scream he drove his heel into the mud, sprang forward and brutally plunged the spear into the bound man's thigh.

Marg was guilty.

The driving rain stung Marg's flesh as they dragged him, bleeding, from the rock. He struggled briefly, but it was hopeless. They raised him onto their shoulders and ran with him down to the edge of the peat bog. They were laughing now. They swung him once. Marg tried to cry out. They swung him twice. He closed his eyes. And as they swung him for a third time and let him go, dropping him like a stone into the middle of the deadly, sucking peat, he vowed with all the strength left in his body that one day he would find these men and take his revenge on them. Then the bog closed over his head and he was gone.

"Helen! Helen! Where are you?" The sound of dish washing carried up the stairs as clearly as a rifle shot. Helen sat tight.

"Helen, will you come downstairs this instant and help me dry these breakfast things!"

She turned the page of her comic and blocked her ears with loo paper.

Helen was a bit of a shirker. Every day her mother would ask her to help clear the table and every day she said she'd love to, but she just had to go to the loo first.

"Why is it," said her mother, "that whenever there's work to be done in this house, you always have to go upstairs?"

"Yes," added Damien, her elder brother, "and leave ME to do it all by myself."

Helen hurled herself at Damien and beat him feverishly about the head with her cereal spoon.

"If I didn't go to the loo I might have an accident," she said, trying to squeeze a couple of crocodile tears from bone-dry eyes.

"If you go to the loo again you *will* have an accident,"

shouted Damien, "'cos I'll pull your head off and bash your brains in!"

"Stop it!" shouted their mother. "Helen, in future, you will stay here until the washing up is finished, because if you don't . . ."

Helen laughed. "If I don't . . . what?" she cheeked.

"Because if you don't, and you continue to spend half your waking hours on the loo then as sure as night turns to day, the Bogman will get you!"

Helen's mother had worked herself up into quite a lather. She struggled to snap off her rubber gloves, hurled the tea towel at Damien and left the kitchen in a flurry of soap suds.

The tap gurgled and spat out a tiny drop of black slime.

"Why don't you listen to anything she says?" said Damien, who was smirking in the corner.

"Did she say Bogman?" asked Helen, who had only been half listening when her mother had exploded. "Who's he?"

Damien assumed an air of annoying superiority. "If you don't listen, you'll never know," he said, slamming the door as he left the room.

"The Bogman," said Helen, rolling the word around her tongue like a gobstopper. "I like the sound of that."

As she spoke a second glob of black slime trickled from the tap and hung like a piece of elastic, bouncing up and down until it snapped.

Helen didn't notice it. She got up, poured her mug of tea into the sink and went out to school, leaving the dregs to congeal and block up the plughole.

In the waste-pipe underneath the plughole something

was dripping, but it was not tea. It was a black sticky substance, like diabolic hair gel, which slithered down the sides of the pipe and trailed off into the cloudy, grey sewer water which flowed below Helen's street.

That night while Helen's father was cooking supper, Helen asked him a question.

"Who's the Bogman?" she said.

"Who?" replied her father. His mind was on the cheese grater.

"Bogman!"

"Oh yes, I think I read about that somewhere," he said. Helen waited. Her father carried on grating.

"Honestly, why can't parents take a little more interest in their children?" Helen thought. She persisted, "*What* have you read about Bogman?"

"Do you want supper or not?" snapped her father.

"Not until you've told me about Bogman."

"Oh all right then," said Helen's father, who had just grated the end off his little finger and was glad of the break. "But not until you STOP rattling that cutlery drawer!"

Helen was slightly surprised at her father's sudden outburst. "I'm not rattling anything," she protested.

Helen's father frowned. He was sure that he had heard a rattling noise. It had sounded like a handful of chopsticks spinning madly in a tumble drier.

There was a slight pause, while Helen studied her father's confusion. When she judged the moment to have passed, she tugged at his apron.

"Go on, then," she said. "Tell me about the Bogman."

Helen's father blinked and muttered, "Oh yes." Then added, more firmly. "Six months ago, when they were building that new sewage works up the road, some workmen dug up a skeleton."

"A live one?"

Helen's father looked at her curiously. "Sometimes," he said, "I wonder if God forgot to include the batteries for your brain. Honestly . . . a *live* skeleton!"

"I was only asking," said Helen.

"No, it was not live. In fact it was very dead. Had been for over two and a half thousand years. They reckon it was the skeleton of some poor chap who was killed in the Stone Age."

"So how come he was still there, then?"

"The peat bog," said Helen's father. "It preserved him in almost perfect condition."

"Oh," said Helen. "So why did Mum tell me that if I spend too much time on the loo the Bogman will get me?"

"It's just a story," said her father. "They say that this skeleton is wandering through the sewers looking for the men who drowned him in the bog."

"Has he found them?"

"Of course not. They died over two thousand years ago as well."

"So why might he attack me?"

"Because you spend too much time in the lavatory when you should be helping your mother!" said her father. "Now can I please get back to my cauliflower cheese?"

Cauliflower cheese and jam sponge. The meal was a

family favourite, and they sat in silence, shovelling down great wadges of it. The only problem with cauliflower cheese and jam sponge is that it does not magically cook itself. On the draining board stood a mountain of dirty pans and dishes. Helen took one look and got up from the table.

"Just got to go to the loo," she declared, as she beat a hasty retreat towards the door.

"Not so fast," said her father, who was having difficulty keeping his eyes open. "What about the washing up?"

"I'll do it when I get back," Helen lied. She saw her father's eyes suddenly slam shut.

"Brian!" scolded Helen's mother. "For once in your life, behave like her father!" But it had no effect. Helen's father, exhausted by the hard work involved in preparing and devouring such a huge supper, had fallen asleep, face down, in the remains of his custard. Helen seized the opportunity and made good her escape.

She reached the landing in double quick time, hurtled into the loo and bolted the door behind her. Now she could read her comic. The one she had secretly stashed away behind the cistern. She sat on the loo and rapidly became engrossed.

A strange rattling noise broke the silence. That would be her mother doing the dishes, thought Helen, and she carried on reading. Then she heard it again, only this time it was closer and it definitely wasn't dishes. Dishes didn't have feet and she could hear footsteps. It was coming from underneath her, from inside the loo. She jumped off and lifted the seat. It looked normal enough, just like loos always look. Pretty boring in fact. But there was that noise again.

Rattling footsteps and a low rhythmical moaning that sounded like an animal in distress.

A sharp blast of icy wind whistled under the door and Helen felt something wet on her cheek. It was a drop of rain. She looked up and saw a heavy black thunder cloud hanging over the light bulb. Suddenly it went dark. The rain came faster now and lashed against her face and arms. A foul smell of rotting wood filled her nostrils. She shouted out, "What do you want?"

And the voice replied, "I want my revenge."

Downstairs, Helen's mother was trying to do the washing up, but something strange was happening. Black sticky goo was bubbling out of her taps, filling the sink, and running down her easy-wipe kitchen unit onto the floor. Damien was giggling again. Helen's father was still asleep.

From the depths of the U-bend came a fearsome cry that turned Helen to stone. She knew what was happening. She knew what was down that pan!

"I'll do the washing up," she bleated, hoping that this might appease the demonic force that was out to get her.

Five boney fingers suddenly shot round the bend, and burst out of the water. A huge explosion ripped the cistern off the wall. Helen was sent spinning backwards by the jet of water spurting from the ruptured pipe. She wiped the water from her eyes and screamed.

"I am Marg," said the skeleton, who had just come up through the loo.

"And I am Helen," wept Helen, as the skeleton's fingers closed around her arm.

Helen's father woke with a start. By now, the black sticky stuff had not only filled up most of the kitchen, but it had also oozed down inside his trousers. He squelched to his feet and frantically tried to bale it out through the back door with a saucepan.

"What is it?" shouted Helen's mother.

"I don't know," he shouted back. "It looks like peat!"

Damien stopped giggling.

"Helen!" he yelled. "Helen's upstairs by herself!"

But of course Helen was not by herself.

"You're the Bogman!" she stammered.

"Your mother called me," hissed the skeleton.

"She was making it up! She didn't know you were real. She just wanted me to do the washing up!"

"And your father knows who killed me!"

"No," pleaded Helen. "He's just my *dad*!"

"You come with me!" cried Bogman, grabbing Helen by her hair and dragging her back towards the loo.

Helen struggled, pathetically. "I can't swim," she blubbed. "Don't throw me in the sewers!" But the skeleton was in no mood for feeble excuses.

"You must die," he moaned. "Then your parents are sure to tell me where I can find my killers!"

As the first hair on Helen's head touched the churning fountain of peat and sewage, the loo door burst open. A flash of lightning sparked across the light bulb and Marg twisted round to face Helen's parents.

"Where are my killers?" he said, stretching out his boney fingers towards Helen's mother's throat.

"It's Bogman!" shouted Helen.

Helen's mother screamed as Bogman's laughing white teeth flashed towards her. Damien ran into his bedroom and locked the door. Helen rolled up her comic and threw it to her father. Her father brought it crashing down on Marg's head.

Only it wasn't a comic. It was a spear. A Stone Age spear.

The skeleton crumbled under the weight of the heavy wooden shaft. The thunder cloud rolled away and the loo stopped bubbling black peat.

Marg's powdered remains floated to the ground as dust. They settled on the thick carpet of soggy peat, and very slowly sank, just as Marg had done two thousand years before, in the peat bog.

Helen looked at her parents. Her father was staring blankly at his empty hands. The Stone Age spear had vanished, just as mysteriously as it had appeared in the first place. Her mother had her head in her hands and was weeping. The house was in an awful mess. It took the family three weeks to clear it up, but for once Helen did not have to be asked to help. In fact she shovelled more peat than anyone else.

Marg never found the six men who killed him. He was swept up with the peat and thrown onto the back of a dustcart. And that, you might think, was that. You may be right, but who's to say that Bogman won't come back to find his killers? I, for one, am not brave enough to make such a prediction. After all, he survived for two thousand years in a peat bog, and now all that holds him is a black plastic bin liner and a few tons of earth, down at Helen's local rubbish tip.

He may yet return.

The Broken-Down Cottage

There are good ghosts and bad ghosts, just as there are good children and bad children. The difference is that bad ghosts are always bad, but bad children can sometimes get better.

Augustus Filch was a bad child. He had run away from home. He didn't like his parents, because they were always telling him what to do. He didn't like his teachers either, because they would shout at him when he talked in class. And he didn't like his friends, because they didn't like him. In fact they weren't really friends at all. So he packed a carrier bag full of toys, put a chocolate biscuit in his pocket and stole enough money from his mother's purse to take a bus ride into the countryside.

It was raining as he got down from the bus. The doors hissed shut behind him and the back of the bus disappeared into the middle of a swirling cloud of thick grey mist. Augustus pulled his school blazer tightly round his neck. It was freezing cold and he had no idea where he was. In the distance he could see a light. Somebody had obviously watched him get down off the bus, and had switched on a light to guide him through the fog.

As he set off towards the light, Augustus shouted out, "This is the life!" to cheer himself up, but he didn't mean it.

He walked fast, for fear of what might be lurking in the bushes on either side of him, and it wasn't long before he saw the faint outline of a small broken-down cottage. Smoke rose from the chimney and curled upwards in a twisting spiral, before spreading out and disappearing into the mist. Somebody was at home.

"Ow!" Augustus yelped. He had stubbed his toe on an old piece of wood that was lying on the track. He picked it up and read the words which were engraved on the wood. It was the name of the cottage: "Dun' Inn".

Augustus knocked twice on the front door and waited, hopping nervously from foot to foot. Nobody came. He knocked again. Somebody had put the light on, so there had to be somebody in – that was the usual way of things.

"Maybe this cottage is not usual," thought Augustus suddenly. He had to admit that it was most odd that nobody had appeared to find out what all the knocking was about.

The front door was not locked. Augustus put his shoulder against it and shoved. At first it would not move, but gradually the rusty hinges gave way and the wooden door creaked open. Inside, the floor was covered in a deep carpet of dust. Cobwebs hung from the ceiling and a bat, disturbed by the noise, flew over Augustus' head and out of the cottage.

THE BROKEN-DOWN COTTAGE

"Nice," thought Augustus. "This is just what I was looking for!" But again, he didn't mean it.

A roaring fire threw flickering shadows onto the ceiling. They bowed towards Augustus and beckoned him forward. As he moved into the room he heard a noise in the corner. It was a rocking chair, rocking very slowly, just as it would have done if Augustus' grandfather had been sitting in it, smoking his pipe.

"Grandpa?" said Augustus nervously. "Grandpa?"

"Augustus," said a voice behind him.

"Grandpa. It is you," shouted Augustus, and he spun round to where the voice had come from. There was nobody there.

"I'm over here," said the voice again, and a boney hand tapped Augustus on the shoulder. He went as white as a sheet. There was someone breathing on the back of his neck.

"Aren't you going to turn round, Augustus?"

Augustus shook his head.

"I won't bite," said the voice softly in his ear.

Augustus screwed up his eyes and slowly turned round.

"See," said the scruffy little boy who was standing in the room with Augustus. "I'm your friend."

The boy's name was Arthur. He had run away from home, too, many years before.

"I like it here," said Arthur. "I can do what I like and nobody tells me off! There's only one problem."

"What's that?" said Augustus, who was eating the chocolate biscuit, and wishing he had stolen six. (He was *that* hungry.)

"I think this cottage is haunted!"

A biscuit crumb quivered on Augustus' bottom lip. "You mean, g . . . g . . . g . . . ghosts?" he stammered.

Augustus looked nervously at the winding staircase that led upstairs to the bedrooms.

"Not *just* ghosts," replied Arthur, "BAD ghosts!"

Augustus choked. He had eaten the biscuit wrapper by mistake.

"They come in the dead of night, with chains and axes, and wail by your bedside. They scratch and scrape at the cellar door and beg you to release them. And if you go to sleep, they enter your dreams and fill your head with wicked thoughts."

"I think I'll go home now," said Augustus.

"And leave me here all by myself?" said Arthur. "You can't. Stay for tonight and we'll have some fun."

Augustus was easily persuaded. Arthur assured him that the ghosts would not trouble them if they stuck together, and it had been so long since Arthur had played with someone of his own age that Augustus felt sorry for him. Besides Arthur had promised Augustus that they would get up to no end of mischief, and any boy who is wicked enough to run away from his parents cannot refuse an offer like that. Augustus stayed.

The two boys sat in the rocking chair and thought up terrible things to do. Augustus had a hundred ideas. They could go back to the road where the bus had stopped and shout names at passing cyclists. They could catch flies and drown them in the sink. They could find a dirty puddle and fill their boots with mud. They could refuse to eat their food, (but as Arthur pointed out, they only had one chocolate biscuit between them, and Augustus had already eaten that).

"We could have a pillow fight!" shouted Augustus, who was getting carried away with excitement.

"Boring!" yawned Arthur. "When I said have some fun, I meant some *real* fun. Let's dial 999 and tell the police that there's a burglar in the house."

"Way to go!" shouted Augustus. "I'll make it look like there's been a robbery and you make the phone call."

They had just finished tying themselves up when three snarling police dogs leapt through the window and knocked them to the ground.

A large pair of black boots scuffed up the dust under Augustus' nose and made him sneeze.

"Good evening, sir," said a gruff voice. "Are you a burglar?"

"No," replied Arthur, trying not to laugh. It was difficult with three alsatians licking his face.

"Then would you mind telling me who is?"

"I'm not entirely sure, officer. You see . . . erm . . . my friend made the phone call."

The policeman yanked Augustus up by the seat of his trousers. Augustus' sides were splitting, but he dared not let the policeman see.

"And do you know who the burglar is, sir?"

"Me, I suppose," howled Augustus, for whom all of this was too much. Both he and Arthur collapsed on the floor in helpless giggles.

The policeman took a deep breath, then pressed his bristly face up close to Augustus.

"Do this again, son, and I'll lock you up for five years,"

he said. Then with a loud command of "Down, Fang, down!" he stormed out of the cottage.

It took the two boys half an hour to calm down. The policeman's face had been the funniest thing they had ever seen.

"Let's do it again!" shouted Augustus. Arthur had already picked up the receiver.

"Ambulance, please," he said. "As soon as possible. My friend's in a terrible state of shock!"

Augustus grabbed the receiver and put on his illest voice. "Help!" he moaned.

"Quick! Quick!" shouted Arthur. "I think he's seen a ghost!"

He slammed the receiver down and burst out laughing.

Augustus pulled his shirt tails out and ran around the room making loud "Whooooo! Whooooo! Whooooo" noises.

They heard the ambulance screech to a halt outside. They heard shouting and doors banging. Augustus pulled his hair up straight and fell to the floor in a pretend dead feint.

Then two ambulancemen beetled in carrying a stretcher.

"Who's seen a ghost?"

"He has," shouted Arthur. "It was huge and had enormous teeth and a beating stick, and green toes."

Augustus's belly wobbled. If he didn't laugh soon he would die.

The ambulanceman knelt down and cradled Augustus's head in his hands. "Are you all right, son?"

"No" whimpered Augustus, "I think I'm dying!"

"Quick," shouted the ambulanceman. "The big needle.

Now!"

Miraculously Augustus was cured. "I'm awake," he shouted. "I'm all right! I don't need the big needle!"

The ambulanceman stood up and walked to the door without saying a word. Just before he left, he turned round.

"Remember, boys," he said, "next time, when you really are in trouble, we won't turn up. You'll have to get better all by yourselves!"

Arthur was straight back on the phone, the moment the ambulanceman had left.

Ten minutes later the air was filled with the sound of clanging bells as three fire engines screeched to a halt outside the cottage. There was a thump on the door and five huge firemen burst into the room.

"Where's the fire?" shouted their chief.

Augustus was piling wood onto the open fireplace.

"Here," he said.

"Come on, laddie! WHERE'S THE FIRE!" shouted the Fire Chief again.

"Here!" said Augustus. "Do you want to warm your tootsies by it?"

Arthur sniggered. Augustus snorted and pretended it was a cough. The Chief's face turned red. The veins stood out on his forehead.

"NO FIRE!"

"Not really," cheeked Augustus. The Fire Chief lifted him up by his ears. "You may think that ringing the Fire Brigade and shouting "Fire!" is funny, but I don't. If you ever waste our time again, I'll give you such a walloping, that I will start a fire! On your bottom!"

Then he dropped Augustus onto the floor, turned round and led his men out of the cottage.

Augustus and Arthur wept with the sheer brilliance of what they had done. In fact they cried themselves to sleep with laughter, in front of the roaring log fire.

When they woke in the morning, they were both cold.

"Let's phone someone else," said Augustus.

"Can't think of anyone," replied Arthur, who had gone off the idea.

"How about our parents? They could come and get us."

"My parents wouldn't come out here to rescue me," said Arthur, sadly.

"Mine would, if we told them that this cottage was haunted by a twelve headed dog with fangs the size of daggers, and that we were really really scared!" shouted Augustus, rushing to the phone.

Half an hour later Augustus's parents got down off the bus and ran towards the black smoke coming from beyond the trees. As they got closer to the cottage, they smelled the fire. When the cottage came into view, they saw for themselves the charred skeleton, the smouldering remains of the broken down cottage.

The Fire Chief was standing by the front door.

"What's happened?" said Augustus's father.

"Two young tearaways mucking about," said the Chief. "Must have fallen asleep in front of the fire. Probably a log, rolling off onto the carpet."

"But they just phoned us up. Told us to come and get them. There's a twelve headed hound from Hell in there!"

"That sounds like them, all right," said the policeman, who was standing next to the Fire Chief.

"Augustus!"

Augustus's mother was running. "Augustus!" She shouted out her little boy's name for a second time. She had reached the door before anyone could stop her. She was expecting to find two burnt bodies, but as she slipped inside, her look of terror turned to one of joy. She was wrong. Augustus and Arthur were standing by the fireplace.

"Hi, mum," said Augustus. "Am I glad to see you. We were absolutely terrified last night! There were hundreds of ghosts!"

"Where?" said his mother.

"Here," said Augustus.

"Here?" said Augustus's mother. "Well, what did they look like?"

"A bit like us," said Augustus and Arthur together.

Then they both walked out of the cottage through the solid stone wall.

Guilt Ghost

There was a fight in a bar. One man got so angry with another man that he hit him hard on the chin. The other man went down like a sack of red mullet. He hit his head on the leg of a table and died. The man who had punched him was so scared by what had happened, that he ran out of the bar and did not stop running until he had worn out the soles on his shoes. When he did stop, he stopped for good. He was far enough away from the bar for no one to recognise him. So he bought a house, got a job and started a new life with people who didn't know that he had killed another man.

He, alone, knew his dark secret.

For several months the man lived contentedly, trying to forget about the fight in the bar. He might have succeeded too, if one morning he had not woken up to find a ghost in his newspaper. It was tiny. No bigger than a full stop. It jumped off the page, onto his cereal spoon, across his bowl of milky flakes, up his tie, across his nose, and settled down, as comfortably as it could, behind his ear.

"You killed a man," whispered the ghost.

"Sssh," said the man. "Nobody must know."

"But killing's wrong."

"I know that!" replied the man.

"Then you should be punished," insisted the ghost.

"Shut up," shouted the man. "I don't want to hear this!"

For three months the ghost sat behind the man's ear and would not let him forget his terrible misdeed.

Then one day there was a knock at the man's door. A policeman was standing outside. He had a silver badge in one hand and a gun in the other.

"Can I come in?" said the policeman.

"Yes," said the man.

"Do you know anything about the death of this man?" said the policeman, proffering a photograph of the man who had died in the bar.

The ghost popped his head round the man's ear and whispered, "Go on. Admit that you killed him. You know you want to."

"No," said the man, handing the photograph back. "I have never seen this man before in my life."

The tiny ghost started to grow the moment that this lie had passed the man's lips. The ghost was soon the size of a parrot and it sat on the man's shoulder.

"Why did you lie?" said the ghost.

"Why've you grown?" said the man.

"Oh, I can get much bigger than this," replied the ghost. "It depends how long you're planning to take before you tell the truth."

"Never!" said the man.

"Then I shall be with you for the rest of your life," said the ghost, smiling, "and I'll probably end up the size of a church."

It was uncomfortable for the man to sleep, with a ghost the size of a parrot perched on his shoulder. He became tired and bad tempered. He blamed everything on his ghost.

"If you weren't there," he'd say, "I wouldn't feel so terrible all the time."

"That's exactly why I am here."

"Why?" questioned the man.

"To make you feel terrible," said the ghost. "You've done a terrible thing and don't deserve to feel good about it."

"How many times do I have to tell you," shouted the man. "It was an accident."

"Accident Schmaccident!" pooped the ghost. "You killed a man with your bare hands, and there's an end to it."

When the man opened the door and saw two silver badges and two guns, he was twice as nervous as before. The policeman had returned with a colleague.

"I won't keep you long," said the policeman. "Do you recgonise this?"

It was the man's scarf. He had dropped it in the bar, on the night of the fight, but had been too scared to go back and get it.

"Of course he does!" said the ghost. But the policeman couldn't see or hear the ghost, so he just stood his ground and waited for an answer.

"No," lied the man. "I have never seen that scarf before in my life."

As the policeman turned to leave, the parrot-sized ghost grew for a second time. It was the size of a crocodile now. It slithered off the man's shoulder and crawled around his feet, whispering words that the man didn't want to hear, and tripping him up wherever he went.

At a party, a woman asked him what he did for a living.

"He kills people," said the ghost on the floor. "He breaks their jaws and splits their heads in two."

"Shut up!" hissed the man.

"Charming," said the woman.

"No. Not you," said the man. "I was talking to my . . . er . . . my . . ."

How do you explain a ghost? How can you expect a person to believe that you are not mad when you tell them that a crocodile-sized ghost lives under your feet, and

talks to you. You can't. The man gave up and left the party.

"You're ruining my life!" said the man to his ghost when they got home.

"Not me," replied the ghost. "It wasn't me who got into a fight. I'm just here as a constant reminder that it was you."

"I don't need reminding!" shouted the man.

"When you tell the truth, I'll be gone," said the ghost. "In the meantime, shove up!"

Then he curled himself around the man's ankles and went to sleep.

When the policeman came back for a third time, the man looked terrible. He had not slept for a week. The ghost had not stopped talking.

"Don't forget you killed a man," the ghost would say.

"Don't forget *that*, whatever you do. You took another man's life. They'll get you in the end. You deserve to be punished. You know you do. Just get it over with, tell the policeman the truth!"

"Well?" said the policeman. "You can't deny that the fingerprints are a perfect match. Did you kill the other man?"

The man took a deep breath. Tiny beads of perspiration glistened on his unshaven top lip. He wrung his hands and looked down at his ghost. "No," he said, "I have never killed another man in my life."

This was the biggest lie of them all. The ghost twitched at his feet. Then it rolled away, across the room, in a fiery ball of twisting limbs. The crocodile skin cracked and fell away. The ghost was changing again, only, this time it was not getting any bigger. This time it was covered in soft, pink skin. This time it had a face. The man's face. And the policeman could see him.

"I'll ask you again," said the policeman to the ghost. "Did you kill the other man?"

"I did," said the ghost.

Then the ghost was lead away by the police, leaving the man alone in his house. The man could not believe what had happened. It didn't make sense. The ghost had taken the blame for his crime, yet had left him to carry on with his life as normal.

He went into the kitchen to get himself a beer, but when he tried to open the refrigerator, his fingers went straight through the handle.

The man and his ghost had swapped places. For good.

GUILT GHOST

A Lesson from History

It was History. Elisa hated History. She had never known much, and now that it was time for her to sit an exam she knew even less.

"Who was shot in the eye with an arrow?" said her best friend Rachel as they waited outside the exam hall.

"I don't know," said Elisa anxiously. "Are you sure this is History."

"Yes, it was Harold," said Rachel.

"Harold who?" said Elisa.

"Harold the king."

"Never heard of him," sulked Elisa. "It's a stupid name for a king anyway."

"Don't you know anything?" laughed Rachel.

"Not much," said Elisa. "I know when I was born."

"That doesn't count."

"I wish it did," said Elisa.

But she had only herself to blame. Elisa had not done a stroke of work in the last year. She had been far too busy hanging around coffee shops and eating huge chocolate eclairs to spend any time swotting up on History. Unfortunately, exams have an unpleasant knack of finding such things out.

Miss Panine de Burm, the French teacher who was invigilating the exam, appeared from inside the Hall. "We're ready for you now, girls," she said.

Elisa cringed. She was going to fail, she knew it.

They filed into the exam hall like a pack of frightened lemmings rushing towards the edge of a cliff. Heads down, palms sweating, lucky mascots clutched feverishly to their breasts. (I have never actually seen a lemming on the edge of a cliff, clutching a lucky mascot to its breast, but I have it on good authority that the majority of them do. Gonks with green hair are a particular favourite, I believe). If fear could be bottled and sold for lots of

113

money in the shops, then the place to start bottling it would surely have been the school hall where Elisa and Rachel were about to sit their history exam.

"You have exactly three hours to complete your paper," declared Miss Panine de Burm, when they had all found their seats and laid out their pens and pencils in regimented lines. "You may look at the questions . . . MAINTENANT!" There was a flurry of activity as one hundred and fifty pieces of paper were turned at the same time. Then there was one minute of complete silence while one hundred and fifty pairs of eyes scanned the questions. Then there was another frantic commotion as one hundred and forty nine girls unscrewed their pen tops and started writing. The one hundred and fiftieth girl looked at the others and bit her lip.

"Crikey," she thought, "I wish I'd done a bit more homework!"

Elisa could not answer even one of the fourteen questions.

In such circumstances one must remain calm. Elisa read the questions for a second time and sat back to think deeply. Then she sat forward and leant on her elbows. She gazed at the ceiling, out of the window, at everyone else scribbling madly, then back at the exam paper. Then she had an idea. She read the questions again, just in case they had miraculously changed since she had last looked. They hadn't. Of course they hadn't! They looked just as impossible now as they had five minutes before. Perhaps it was her pen that was stopping her from knowing the answers. She swapped it from her right hand to her left. No difference. She put the lid in her mouth and waited for inspiration, but sadly it didn't come. So, she put the nib in her mouth and covered her lips with blue ink. She hadn't meant to do that. That was stupid. Still, it gave her something to do for the next ten minutes, as she tried to rub the ink off her tongue.

Rachel, who seemed to be writing faster than anyone else, looked up from her paper, and gave Elisa the thumbs up. Elisa had never before hated anyone quite as much as she hated Rachel at that moment. Smug friends who knew the answers were no friends of Elisa. They were just swots. Teachers' Pets, who deserved to have their knickers run up the flagpole in front of the whole school.

"Elisa," said a voice.

Elisa looked up sharply and whipped her legs off the desk.

"Yes, Miss de Burm," she said.

But Miss de Burm was at the other end of the hall, walking in the other direction.

"Elisa!" said the voice again.

"What?" replied Elisa in a loud whisper.

"Over here," said the voice.

Elisa turned to where the voice had come from. The Fire Exit doors stood ajar, and poking her head through the gap was a little girl with short black hair and freckles. She was wearing a brown pinafore dress, black woollen stockings and a pair of lace-up bootees.

"I'm Penny," said the girl with freckles.

"I'm Elisa," said Elisa.

"What are you doing?" said the newcomer.

"History," said Elisa.

"Yuck!" said Penny. "Do you want any help?"

Miss Panine de Burm's voice boomed out from the front of the hall. "Elisa!"

"Quick! Hide!" said Elisa, pushing Penny underneath her desk. "If Miss de Burm finds you here she'll send you to the Sin Bin."

"Stop talking!" shouted the French teacher.

"Relax," said Penny. "She can't see me!"

"This is no time for jokes," whispered Elisa, who was now in a panic. Miss de Burm was steering a direct course for her desk.

"No, she can't, honest," laughed Penny, as she got up from the floor, waved her arms in the air and sang the bit from *Frère Jacques* about soggy semolina. Miss de Burm was now only feet away. Elisa buried her head in her work and pretended that Penny wasn't there.

"Any more talking and I shall send you to the Headmistress, you naughty girl!" said Miss de Burm, glaring down at Elisa.

Penny had crept behind the teacher's back and was pulling faces. Elisa winced.

"What are you looking at?" said Miss de Burm, turning round sharply. She was staring straight at Penny now. Penny lifted her skirt and showed the teacher her bellybutton.

"Nothing," said Elisa weakly.

"Good," said Miss de Burm, flouncing off down the aisle. "Then get on with your work."

When Elisa opened her eyes, Penny was sitting next to her. She was grinning, mischievously, from ear to ear.

"She *DIDN'T* see you!" exclaimed Elisa.

"I told you she wouldn't," said Penny.

"But why?"

"Because I come from another world," said Penny.

Elisa was not sure what this meant. "You mean you come from another school?"

"No, dunderhead! I'm a ghost!" said Penny.

You could have knocked Elisa down with a feather.

"How long have you been dead?" she said.

"About a hundred years," replied Penny. Then she added, "I used to be a pupil at this school, you know, until it burnt down."

"I didn't know the school had burnt down."

"Oh yes, about a hundred years ago, during exam week."

"Do you mean . . ." Elisa couldn't quite say it. "Do you mean that you, as it were, actually, died in the fire?"

"During the History exam," said Penny.

Elisa pricked up her ears. Penny carried on. "So every year during the History exam, I have to come back here and do a bit of haunting."

"How awful for you," said Elisa.

"Oh I don't know," said Penny. "It could be worse."

"How?" Elisa asked.

"It could be Geography," said the ghost. "I'm useless at Geography." She paused to think. "I'm pretty good at History, though."

"Well you would be," said Elisa, who was getting quite excited as a cheaty sort of thought took shape in her mind. "How many times have you sat this History exam?"

"A hundred, of course!" said Penny. "Do you want me to help you?"

"Not half," shouted Elisa.

Miss Panine de Burm looked round.

"But we'd better do it quietly!"

Elisa sat back and let Penny answer her History exam for her. Penny wrote fast, and with great assurance. With half an hour to spare, she handed the paper back to Elisa and announced that she had finished.

"You're brilliant," squealed Elisa.

"I'm exhausted," said Penny. "See you next year."

Then she stood up and disappeared back through the Fire Exit whence she had come.

A week later the exam results were pinned to the notice board. Elisa was bursting to know how she had done. If Penny had sat the exam one hundred times before, it was a cast iron certainty that Elisa was going to come top. A crowd had gathered in front of the results board. Elisa shoved her way to the front and cast her eyes up to the top of the list.

FIRST PLACE: Rachel Smith 98%, it said.

So she hadn't come first. Elisa was a little disappointed, but second place would do.

SECOND PLACE: Tania Wilkins 91%.

She wasn't second either. In fact she wasn't third, fourth, fifth or even sixth. Right at the bottom, in last place, she read the impossible.

THIRTY SECOND PLACE: Elisa Macgregor 0%.

Elisa was stunned. It hadn't crossed her mind that Penny's ghost might be just as lazy and stupid as she was.

Unfortunately, though, it was.

The Ghost of Christmas Turkeys Past

Jack loved turkey more than anything else in the world –
roast, boiled, braised, rolled, plumped, thumped, trussed
and even frozen. He couldn't get enough. The only thing
he didn't like was people telling him that if he only ever ate
turkey, then one day he was sure to turn into one. He
didn't believe it was possible.

"Turkeys," he would say, "have a brain the size of a
pea. My brain is the size of the bidet in my mummy's
bathroom, so it wouldn't fit into a turkey's head. I'd be
the only turkey in the shop with a set of gold taps and a
bidet fountain sticking out between my ears! I'd look
stupid!"

Be that as it may, Jack *was* a turkey freak. When his
mother went shopping, he would tag along to check that
she hadn't forgotten what he liked best. If she dared to
dither at any shelf he would quietly prod her in the ribs,
with a wishing bone that he carried for this express
purpose, and whisper confidentially, lest any other

120

customer should overhear him and steal the last one, "Turkeys. Let's go."

He had once caught his mother trying to sneak a large chicken into her trolley, pretending that it was a turkey, but he wasn't fooled. When he pointed out that the label quite clearly said LARGE CHICKEN (DON'T BE FOOLED INTO THINKING THAT THIS IS A TURKEY), his mother had gone as red as a can of tomatoes, and had hurriedly put the chicken back. Turkey connoisseurs, you see, have a parson's nose for the real thing, and nothing but genuine turkey will do.

As a result Jack's family ate turkey, morning, noon and night. Turkey burgers on a slice for breakfast, drumsticks at lunch, sandwiches at tea, and anything left lurking on the carcass for dinner. Jack's appetite was rapacious. Ten minutes before any meal he would bang his knife and fork on the table and switch into hooligan-mode.

"Turrrkey! Ra ra ra! Turrrkey! Ra ra ra! Turkeeeeeeeeeeey!" he would chant, much to his parents' annoyance.

When the food was served he would bury his face in his plate and snuffle and grunt away like a pig in truffles. Before anyone else had finished he would hold up his plate and shout, "MORE!" at the top of his voice.

Generally, he got it.

At night, Jack would go to bed with a smile on his face and dream the dreams of a carnivore. Squadrons of juicy plump turkeys, carrying banners proclaiming "THIS TURKEY BELONGS TO JACK", would swoop out of the sky in glorious technicolour, land in his back garden, pluck out all of their own feathers, open the door to Jack's oven and climb in of their own accord.

I bet you can guess where Jack went on his summer holidays every year . . . You're right, of course, Greece. (You didn't think it was Turkey, did you?). Greece – where the biggest turkeys in Europe live. And I bet you can guess what his favourite time of the year was. Well, it had to be, didn't it? Christmas, when there were more turkeys in the shops than even Jack could eat. He used to sit outside his local butcher's window, gaze fondly at the rows and rows of hairless birds, and write letters to Father Christmas, explaining that he didn't want a bike, and he didn't want a gun, and he didn't want a train set, but he would *love* a turkey!

Jack's father used to write letters to Father Christmas as well. They always said the same thing –

Dear Santa
Mum likes turkey, I like turkey, and I daresay that even you like turkey, BUT NOT EVERY DAY OF THE YEAR! What can we do about Jack? Please help.
love
His concerned father.

One year, on Christmas Eve, Jack was more excited than usual. His mother had bought the biggest turkey he had ever seen for Christmas dinner. It was bigger even than Jack, and had been delivered to the door by three butcher's boys and a fork lift truck. Jack sat staring at this delicious-looking beast while his father prepared the stuffing.

"Yum yum!" he said, as he licked his lips and imagined all those gorgeous smells that went with roast turkey. He closed his eyes, rubbed his tummy and fell backwards off his chair.

At nine o'clock he was prised away from the dead bird and sent upstairs to bed. He hung a pillowcase over the mantelpiece for Father Christmas, and snuggled down to dream of giant turkeys and drumsticks the size of baseball bats.

Jack's father, on the other hand, put on a pair of woolly socks, a thick scarf and a pink bobble hat. He fetched the long ladder from the garage and carried it next door, to where the Ramsbottoms lived.

"Do you think I could sit on your roof for a bit?" he asked a bewildered Mrs Ramsbottom.

"If you must," she replied. Then, she added, "If you don't think I'm rude, may I ask why? What's wrong with your own roof?"

"I might wake Jack," said Jack's father, mysteriously.

"Oh," said Mrs Ramsbottom. Then she smiled a pitying sort of smile. The sort you give to someone you think might be a bit soft in the head. "Help yourself," she said, and she shut the front door.

Jack's father cut an extraordinary picture against the snow-covered roofs, as he clambered up the ladder. His breath poured out of his mouth, like thick, white smoke. He slid across the icy slates, pulled himself up on the television aerial, sat down with his back against the chimney pot, and waited.

When he heard the jangling of the sleigh bells, two hours later, his bottom was frozen solid, and his blue fingers looked like a fistful of curacao-flavoured ice pops.

"Over here!" he shouted, staggering to his feet, and waving his arms above his head. "Stop!"

Father Christmas got the shock of his life, when this strange apparition leapt up in front of his sleigh. He pulled sharply on the reins, and crash-landed his reindeer into the soft snow on the top of the Ramsbottom's roof. There were toys and presents everywhere. They shot forward over Father Christmas's head and landed in a chaotic heap in front of Jack's father.

"Yo ho ho," said Father Christmas. "Very funny! Are you trying to kill me, or something?"

"Sorry," said Jack's father. "I didn't know how else to attract your attention."

"Try phoning, next time," replied the man with the long white beard. "I thought you were a ghost!"

Jack's father felt very foolish. He knew how busy Father Christmas was, and he hadn't meant to cause him any trouble. Now, the extra work involved in picking up the spilled presents was making Father Christmas all hot and bothered.

"Well come on, then, what do you want? I've got work to do!" he shouted.

"I know it sounds silly, but how can I stop Jack from eating so much turkey?"

"Oh," said Father Christmas, feeling in his pocket for a small piece of paper. It was a note. "You must be Jack's father. Still likes his turkey, does he?"

Jack's father nodded.

"Well, I'll see what I can do," said Father Christmas. "I'll arrange a little surprise for Jack tonight. It should do the trick."

"And put him off turkey for good?"

"I certainly hope not!" said Father Christmas.

"What do you mean?" snorted Jack's father. Rudolf, the red nosed reindeer, gave him a funny look.

"I happen to be partial to a lovely bit of turkey, myself," Father Christmas announced. "I wouldn't want to put Jack off such delicious food for good. I'll just give him a fright. Slow him down a bit. He'll still eat turkey, but not quite so often! Now, give us a hand with this tricycle, will you?"

Then the two men loaded up the sleigh and Father Christmas twinkled off into the night. As he went, he let a shower of magic dust slip from a pouch on his belt. It floated downwards through the clouds, and passed straight through the frosted, glass pane of Jack's bedroom window.

Jack was fast asleep. As he dreamt sweet dreams, about twelve plump turkeys pulling Santa's sleigh across a golden moon, the window in his room swung open. A freezing cold wind filled the curtains and blew them towards Jack's bed. They brushed against his cheek, and tickled the backs of his ears, until he woke up, with a start.

"Who's there?" he said sleepily, rubbing his eyes.

Apparently no one. Just the wind, gently fanning the curtains. Jack would have gone back to sleep, had not, at that precise moment, the most extraordinary thing happened. A cluster of stars fell out of the night sky. They twisted and turned as they dropped towards the earth, but as they drew level with Jack's bedroom window, they stopped. They formed themselves into the shape of an arrow and shot in to the centre of the room. Jack's tongue was hanging out of the front of his mouth as the stars melted away to leave, in their stead, a huge, bald turkey.

"Good evening, Jack," said the turkey.

"Wow!" was all that Jack could muster. Then he said, "What happened to your leg?"

"It got cut off," replied the huge, bald, *one-legged* turkey.

"How?" said Jack, who was fascinated.

"Come with me, and I'll show you," said the turkey, taking Jack's hand with one of his wings. "Oh, by the way, I'm the Ghost of Christmas Turkeys Past."

"Hi! I'm Jack," said Jack, and they flew out of the window, with Jack clinging on for dear life.

Jack had never flown with a turkey before. To be honest, the turkey was good, but not that good. When they flew over water, Jack's toes got wet. After a brief plunge through a small forest, Jack re-emerged with some most uncomfortable branches sticking out of his pyjamas, and in one hair-raising incident, which involved trying to fly over the top of the mountain, they actually had to land and walk the last bit, because the turkey was so pooped. Still, a flight with a one-legged turkey is better than no flight at all.

"We're here," announced the Ghost of Christmas Turkeys Past, finally. "Hold on!" He let go of Jack, who fell like a stone towards the grey earth beneath him. Jack screamed. He was sure he was going to die, but, miraculously, his fall was broken by a huge pile of feathers. The turkey landed on his belly and hopped over to join him.

"Well, what do you think of it?" said the Ghost of Christmas Turkeys Past.

"What?" replied Jack.

"This graveyard," said the turkey. "This is where the

remains of every Christmas dinner for the last one hundred and fifty years is buried." Jack was impressed. That was a lot of turkeys.

"I've never thought about what actually happens to the turkeys once I've eaten them," he said.

"No one ever does. But turkeys have got souls just the same as you. Those souls have got to be laid to rest somewhere."

"And so they come here?"

"Not all of us," replied the Ghost of Christmas Turkeys Past, pointing to a large Concrete building in the distance. A flag was flying at half mast on the roof. It read. "HOME FOR RETIRED WAR VETERANS". Several old turkeys were sitting on the terrace in bath chairs. They were wrapped up in tartan blankets.

"Is that where you live," said Jack, "in that Old Turkey's Home?"

The ghost nodded. "Some of us are unlucky. People start to eat us, but their eyes are too big for their stomachs. They take one bite and leave the rest."

"Is that how you lost your leg?" enquired Jack.

"Precisely," said the old turkey. "A little girl took a shine to it, so her father hacked it off. Then she had the audacity to feed it to the dog."

"That's awful," said Jack.

"Yes," said the one-legged turkey. "There was one consolation, though. The dog choked to death on the bone."

Suddenly a loud beating of wings filled the air. Jack looked up and was surprised to see that the sky had turned black. There were hundreds and hundreds of turkeys flying overhead, and each of them was carrying a bundle in its beak. The Ghost of Christmas Turkeys Past sighed and shook his head. "That'll be the first of the Christmas delivery," he said, sadly. On a signal from their leader, the turkeys opened their beaks and scattered their bundles over the graveyard.

It rained dead turkey bones for twenty minutes. Jack and the Ghost of Christmas Turkeys Past stood in the middle of the downpour without saying a word. When the last bone had come to rest at their feet, the turkey said, "Now Jack, after all that you've seen, do you still want to eat turkey meat for Christmas dinner."

Jack thought for a minute. "I'm afraid I do," he said, "'cos I love it!"

The Ghost of Christmas Turkeys Past scooped Jack up under his wing and took off into the sky. As they flew along, Jack asked where they were going, but the turkey said nothing. He was map reading and required all his concentration to work out where he was.

They landed in a farmyard and were met by another turkey. He looked younger than the Ghost of Christmas Turkeys Past, wore a thin moustache on his top beak, carried a swagger cane, and had two legs.

"All right, Christmas Past stand down," said the younger. "Leave him to *me* now!"

Jack turned to thank his one legged friend, but he had gone.

"Eyes right!" shouted the new turkey. "To the Hen House, quick march!" Jack was marched off before he could complain and, very soon, found himself being pushed through a small wooden door into a long, white, brightly lit hut.

"Prisoner! Halt!" screamed the new turkey.

"But I'm not a prisoner . . ." exclaimed Jack.

"Silence in the ranks!" came the reply. "I am the Ghost of Christmas Turkeys Present. You will listen to what I have to say. I will only say it once, so you'd better sharpen up your lug holes and pay attention! Understood?"

Jack was just about to say no, when the Ghost of Christmas Turkeys Present interrupted again.

"Good! Then hear this. Take a look around you. What do you see?"

"Turkeys," said Jack.

"Correct."

"Thousands of them, all squashed together. What are they doing here?"

"Waiting for the butcher's van! What do you *think* they're doing here, HAVING A PARTY!?" The Ghost of Christmas Turkeys Present pushed the wobbly red bit on top of his beak into Jack's face. "Grow up, laddie!" he barked, unpleasantly.

"But they're all in little cages," said Jack, "and they're sitting on top of each other!"

"And they haven't even been introduced properly! I know. It's terrible!"

Jack was feeling a little queasy. "Isn't it a bit unfair keeping them locked up here day and night?" he asked.

"Ah yes, but it wouldn't be Christmas without turkey," sneered the Ghost of Christmas Turkeys Present, frog-marching Jack back outside into the farmyard.

He called Jack to attention and fixed him with his beady stare.

"Seen enough yet, turkey eater?" he snarled. "Still fancy a succulent bit of juicy leg for your Christmas dinner, do you?"

"Oh dear," said Jack, "you're going to hate me for this, I know, but yes! 'Cos whatever you say, whatever you show me, I do so love turkey!"

Steam whistled out of the ears of the Ghost of Christmas Turkeys Present.

'You," he said, "have asked for this!" Then he turned half a step to his left and bellowed in his most frightening voice. "Ghost of Christmas Turkeys Future! One step forward!"

Out from under the shadows of the Hen House, stepped the largest turkey you have ever seen. One hundred and forty pounds of pure muscle. He was wearing a pair of bright green trousers, Doc Martins, a silk shirt, the coolest shades you ever saw and he had a gold ring through his beak.

"I am de turkey of de future," said this hip hop ghost. "Stick with me brother, and I will show you what's goin'

down!" He slapped Jack's hands with his wings. "Gimme five! Let's fly!"

They soared over the countryside at a thousand miles an hour. Cities flashed past in a trice, mountains shrank to molehills as they climbed high into the earth's atmosphere and circled the globe four times in as many seconds. Jack was so scared he couldn't even scream. They raced submarines along the sea bed, hitched a lift from Concorde and nearly crashed into Father Christmas coming far too fast round the corner of Australia.

Jack was surprised to find himself back outside his parents' house when they landed. "You've brought me home," he said.

The Ghost of Christmas Turkeys Future slapped his thigh and roared with laughter.

"Man, this ain't your home. This is your HOUSE, but it ain't your home! We're like one hundred years in the future. This is what Christmas Day's gonna be like in the year 2090. Take a look, man. Take a look!"

Jack climbed up on the window ledge and peered in through the net curtain. He could see a Christmas tree, with fairy lights on it, in the corner of the room. There was holly around the pictures and a piece of mistletoe hung over the door. The table was set for Christmas dinner, with red napkins, crackers, and party hats. The room looked exactly as it had done when Jack went up to bed on Christmas Eve after watching his father stuff the turkey.

"But I don't see what's different," said Jack.

"You will. You will," said the Ghost of Christmas Turkeys Future, clucking with glee.

Suddenly the kitchen door opened. Jack was expecting

to see his mother, so imagine his surprise when a large turkey, wearing an apron, and carrying a silver platter with a lid on it, backed into the room.

"Come along, children!" she shouted. "Christmas dinner is ready!"

Three little turkeys rushed into the room screaming with delight. They were just like Jack, pushing and shoving each other to be first at the food.

"Sit down and behave!" said their mother. "Now then, dear, will you carve?" She was addressing the largest turkey of them all, who had just come in from the garage. Obviously the father.

Jack was feeling sick again. Even if it was the year 2090, it didn't seem right that turkeys were eating other turkeys for Christmas dinner . . . but then they weren't.

As the father lifted the lid off the silver platter, and sharpened his carving knife, Jack screamed. They were eating him. The turkeys were eating Jack for Christmas dinner!

Jack woke up in bed, screaming.

It was Christmas day, but Jack did not eat turkey for dinner. He took one look at the huge beast that his mother had cooked for him and ate sprouts and roast potatoes instead.

"But I thought you liked turkey," said his father, with a smile on his face.

"Not today," said Jack. "Maybe tomorrow."

Jack's father tucked in his napkin, picked up his knife and fork, and sent up a silent thank you to Father Christmas.

Rogues Gallery

THE 7 MOST WANTED GHOSTS IN BRITAIN

1)   **Old Hollow Legs**

Died for a chocolate fudge slice ten years ago. He recently won the "Greediest Ghost in Greenwich" competition, by consuming the entire contents of a children's tea party (table mats and all) in under twelve seconds. Close friends of Old Hollow Legs admit that they don't know where he puts it all, but they do recommend the locking of all fridge freezers when he is in the vicinity.

Next time your tummy rumbles at dinner table, check that it is yours, and not the ghostly gastric juices of Old Hollow Legs. He does like to lurk under tables waiting for scraps.

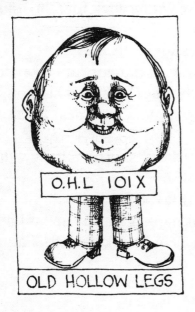

O.H.L 101X

OLD HOLLOW LEGS

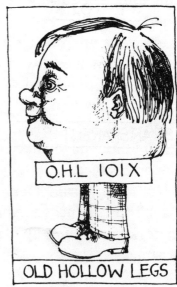

O.H.L 101X

OLD HOLLOW LEGS

2) **Transparent Tony**

When you're at school and tell a whopping great lie to get yourself out of trouble, you probably think you're being clever. In fact, it's not you at all. It's Transparent Tony. He likes to sit in childrens' hair and whisper half-truths in their ears. A word of warning though. Transparent Tony is the worst liar in the whole world, because everyone can see straight through him. So, if you are telling a lie, and you think it's one of Tony's, stop! Nobody will be fooled.

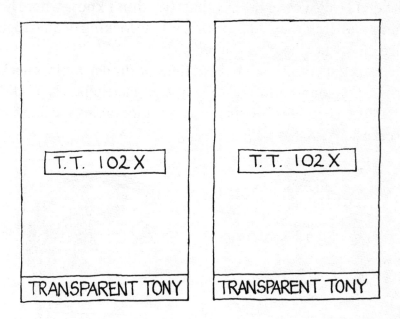

3) **The Headless Coachman**

As his name suggests, the Headless Coachman drives a coach and four horses without a head. Needless to say it took him eighteen attempts before he passed his driving test. Nowadays he just pootles around the M25 and causes the most terrible traffic jams.

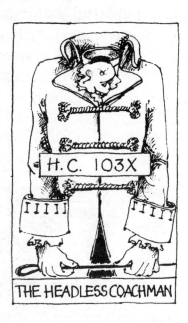 

H.C. 103X
THE HEADLESS COACHMAN

H.C. 103X
THE HEADLESS COACHMAN

4) **The Bermuda Triangle**

Organised crime is not something one usually associates with the Spirit World, but The Bermuda Triangle is a sinister underworld syndicate containing the ghosts of some seven hundred South American gangsters. They meet underwater in boating ponds, and steal children's sailing boats, by sucking them down into the reeds.

A disturbing Police report, published last month, indicates that The Bermuda Triangle may well have turned their attention to remote controlled model aircraft.

You have been warned. If you own a model aeroplane you may already be under surveillance. Beware of low flying ghosts in ponchos!

5)   **Nostalgic Nora**

She's a dear old duck, Nostalgic Nora, but she doesn't
half rabbit on. If you're young, you're quite safe. Nora
isn't interested in you. It's adults that she's interested in.
Nostalgic Nora likes to worm her way inside the minds of
older people and make them talk, for hours and hours on
end, about the past. There's nothing wrong with what she
makes people say, it just happens to be mind-crushingly
boring!

N.N. 105X — NOSTALGIC NORA

6) **The Immortal Remains of Henry Fink**

In 1970 Henry Fink was horribly killed by an axe murderer. His body was chopped into hundreds of little pieces and stored in a large chest freezer. His ghost is similarly disembodied. If Henry Fink comes to your house to do a bit of haunting, you're in for a scarey time. He likes to leave bits of himself scattered around the house. Then, when you open the door, his bits light up. And he smells . . . No. He stinks. His sell by date ran out in 1972!

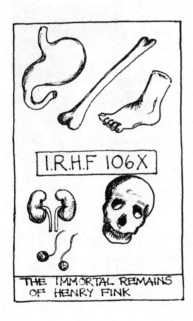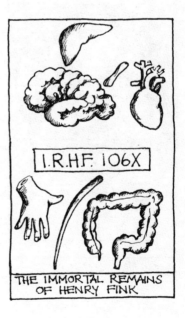

7)   **Smudger**

Who puts chocolate milk stains around your mouth?
Who smears spaghetti bolognaise on your clean, white
tee-shirt? Who rubs grass stains into your knees?
  It's Smudger.
  The grubbiest ghost in the world.

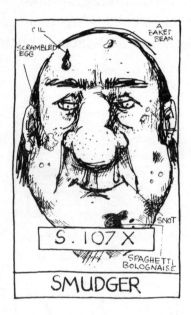 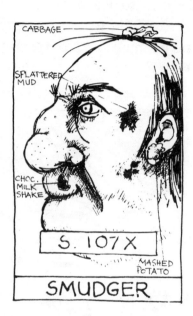